MY BOYFRIEND IS A MONSTER

My Boyfriend Bites

OR

ONCE BITTEN, TWICE SHY

#3

DAN JOLLEY

Illustrated by ALITHA E. MARTINEZ

STORY BY
DAN JOLLEY

ILLUSTRATIONS BY
ALITHA E. MARTINEZ
WITH ADDITIONAL SHADING BY ESTHER SANZ

LETTERING BY
BILL HAUSER

COVER COLORING BY
ELDON COWGUR

Copyright © 2011 by Lerner Publishing Group, Inc.

Graphic Universe™ is a trademark of Lerner Publishing Group, Inc.

Graphic Universe™
A division of Lerner Publishing Group, Inc.
241 First Avenue North
Minneapolis, MN 55401 U.S.A.

Website address: www.lernerbooks.com

Main body text set in CCWildwords. Typeface provided by Comicraft Design.

Library of Congress Cataloging-in-Publication Data

Jolley, Dan.
    My boyfriend bites / by Dan Jolley ; illustrated by Alitha E. Martinez.
       p. cm. — (My boyfriend is a monster ; #03)
    Summary: Seventeen-year-old Vanessa Shingle finds her New Mexico town invaded by vampires and learns it may not be a coincidence that gorgeous Jean-Paul McClelian has turned up in her love life.
    ISBN: 978–0–7613–5599–1 (lib. bdg. : alk. paper)
    1. Graphic novels. [1. Graphic novels. 2. Horror stories. 3. Vampires—Fiction. 4. Vampires—Fiction.
5. New Mexico—Fiction.] I. Martinez, Alitha E., ill. II. Title.
PZ7.7.J65My 2011
741.5'973—dc22
                                      2010028723

Manufactured in the United States of America
1 – BC – 7/15/11

Chapter 1

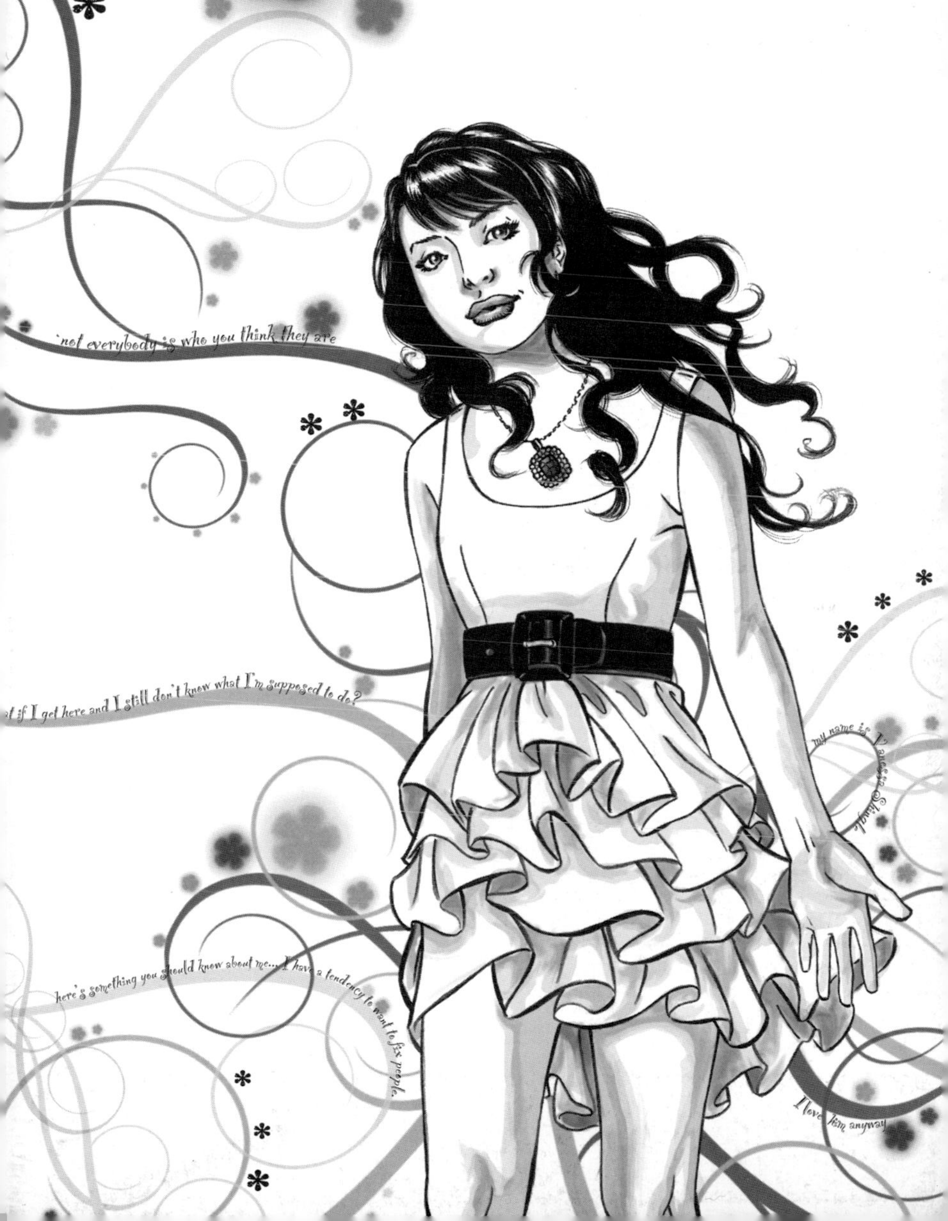

not everybody is who you think they are
t if I get here and I still don't know what I'm supposed to do?
my name is Vanessa Shinple
here's something you should know about me... I have a tendency to want to fix people.
I love him anyway

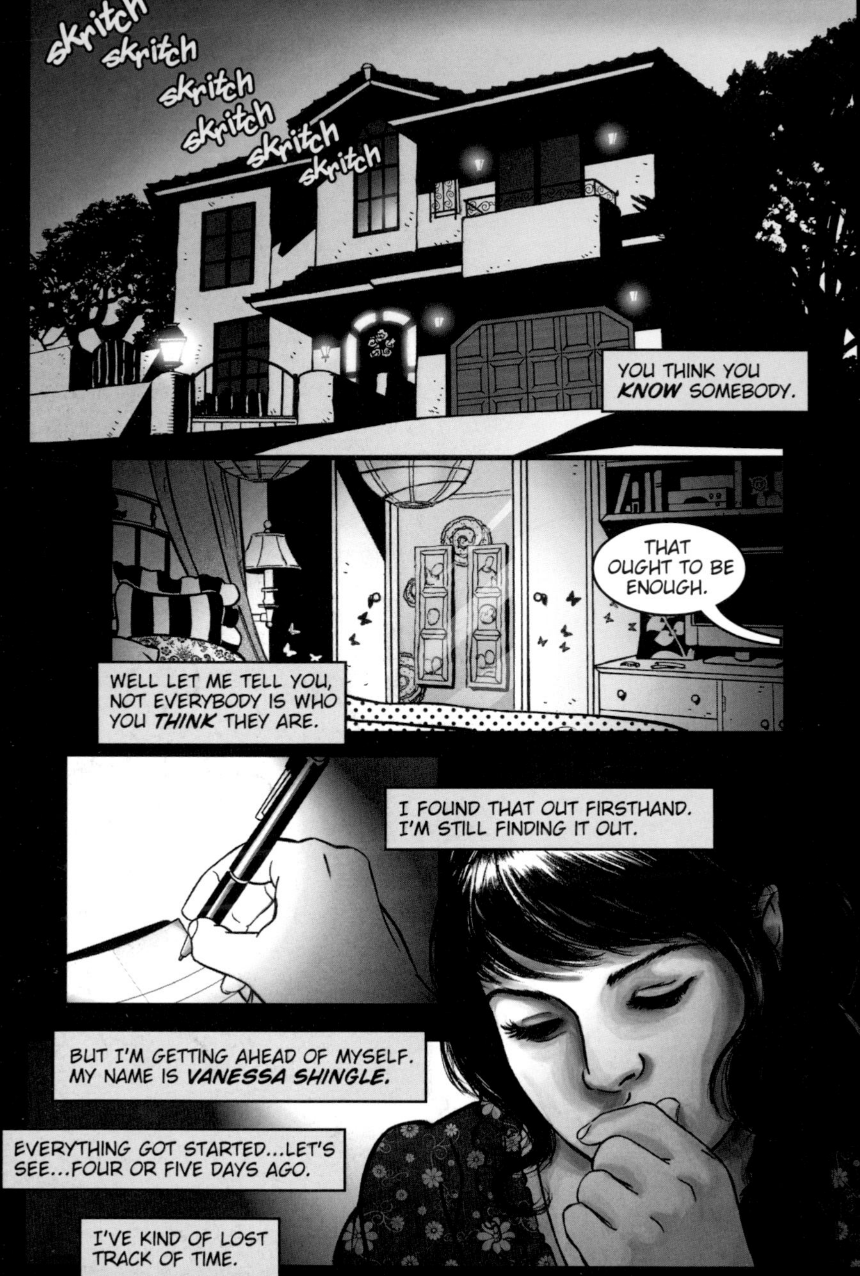
skritch skritch skritch skritch skritch skritch
YOU THINK YOU KNOW SOMEBODY.
THAT OUGHT TO BE ENOUGH.
WELL LET ME TELL YOU, NOT EVERYBODY IS WHO YOU THINK THEY ARE.
I FOUND THAT OUT FIRSTHAND. I'M STILL FINDING IT OUT.
BUT I'M GETTING AHEAD OF MYSELF. MY NAME IS VANESSA SHINGLE.
EVERYTHING GOT STARTED...LET'S SEE...FOUR OR FIVE DAYS AGO.
I'VE KIND OF LOST TRACK OF TIME.

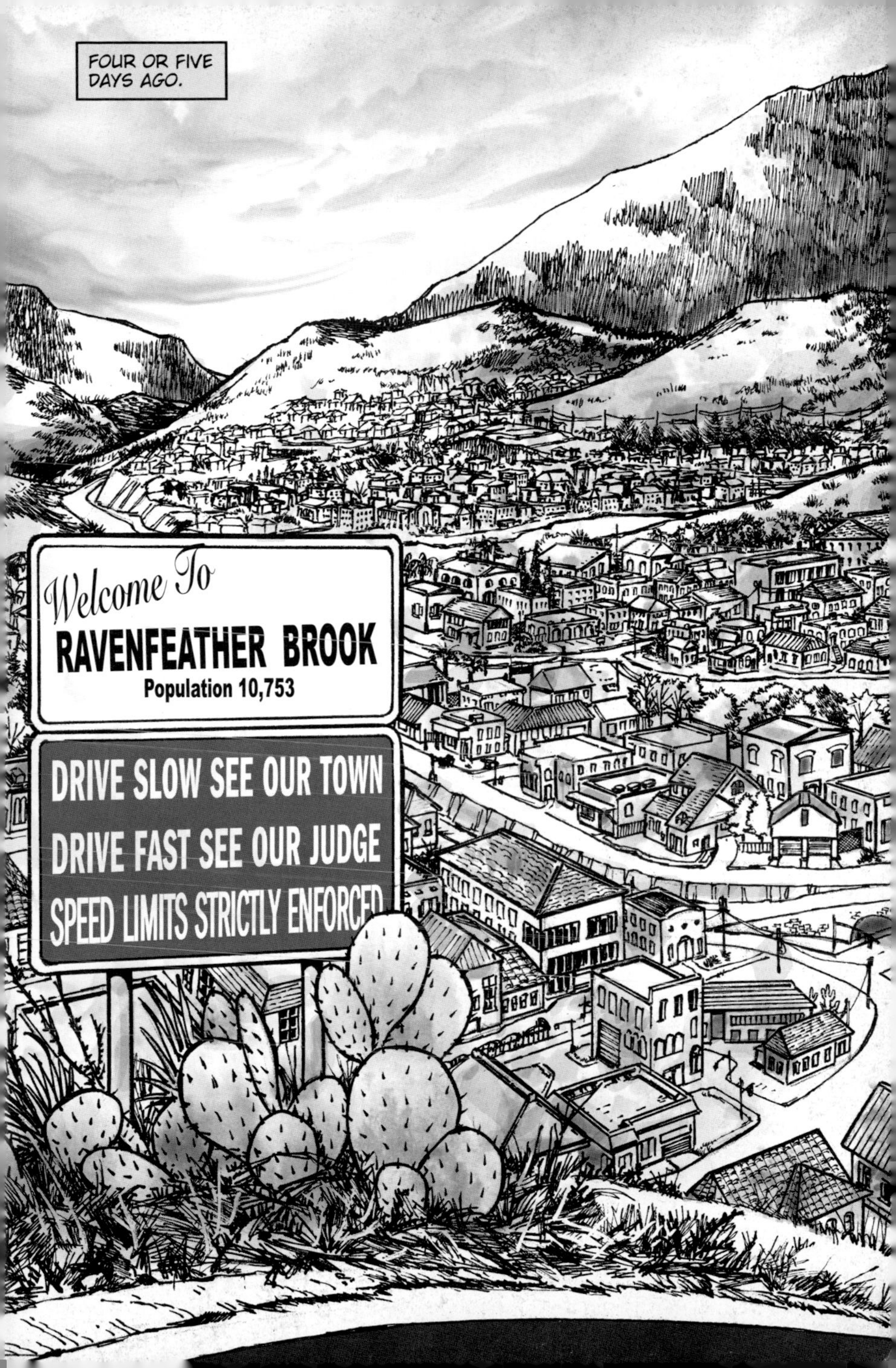
FOUR OR FIVE DAYS AGO.
Welcome To
RAVENFEATHER BROOK
Population 10,753
DRIVE SLOW SEE OUR TOWN
DRIVE FAST SEE OUR JUDGE
SPEED LIMITS STRICTLY ENFORCED

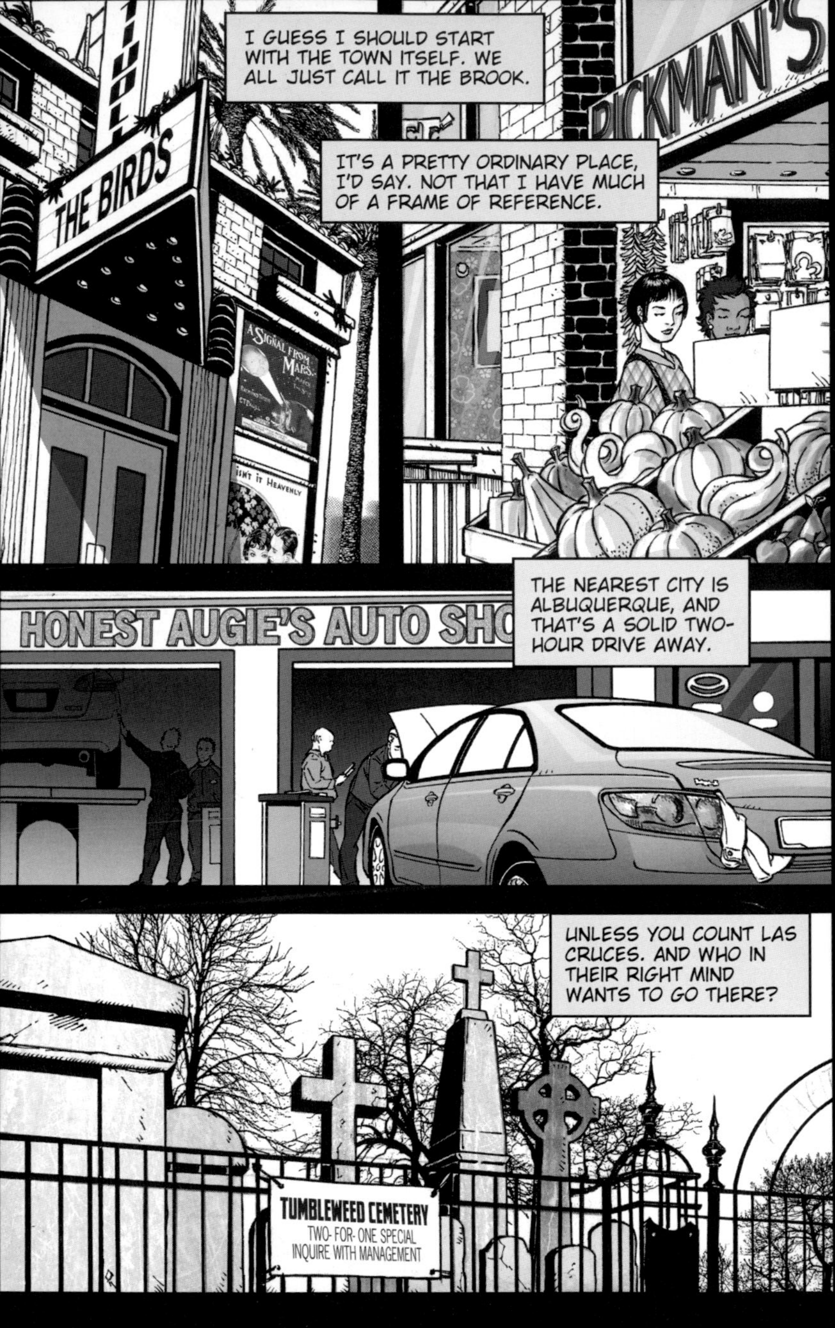
I GUESS I SHOULD START WITH THE TOWN ITSELF. WE ALL JUST CALL IT THE BROOK.
THE BIRDS
IT'S A PRETTY ORDINARY PLACE, I'D SAY. NOT THAT I HAVE MUCH OF A FRAME OF REFERENCE.
A SIGNAL FROM MARS
ISN'T IT HEAVENLY
THE NEAREST CITY IS ALBUQUERQUE, AND THAT'S A SOLID TWO-HOUR DRIVE AWAY.
HONEST AUGIE'S AUTO SHO
UNLESS YOU COUNT LAS CRUCES. AND WHO IN THEIR RIGHT MIND WANTS TO GO THERE?
TUMBLEWEED CEMETERY
TWO- FOR- ONE SPECIAL
INQUIRE WITH MANAGEMENT

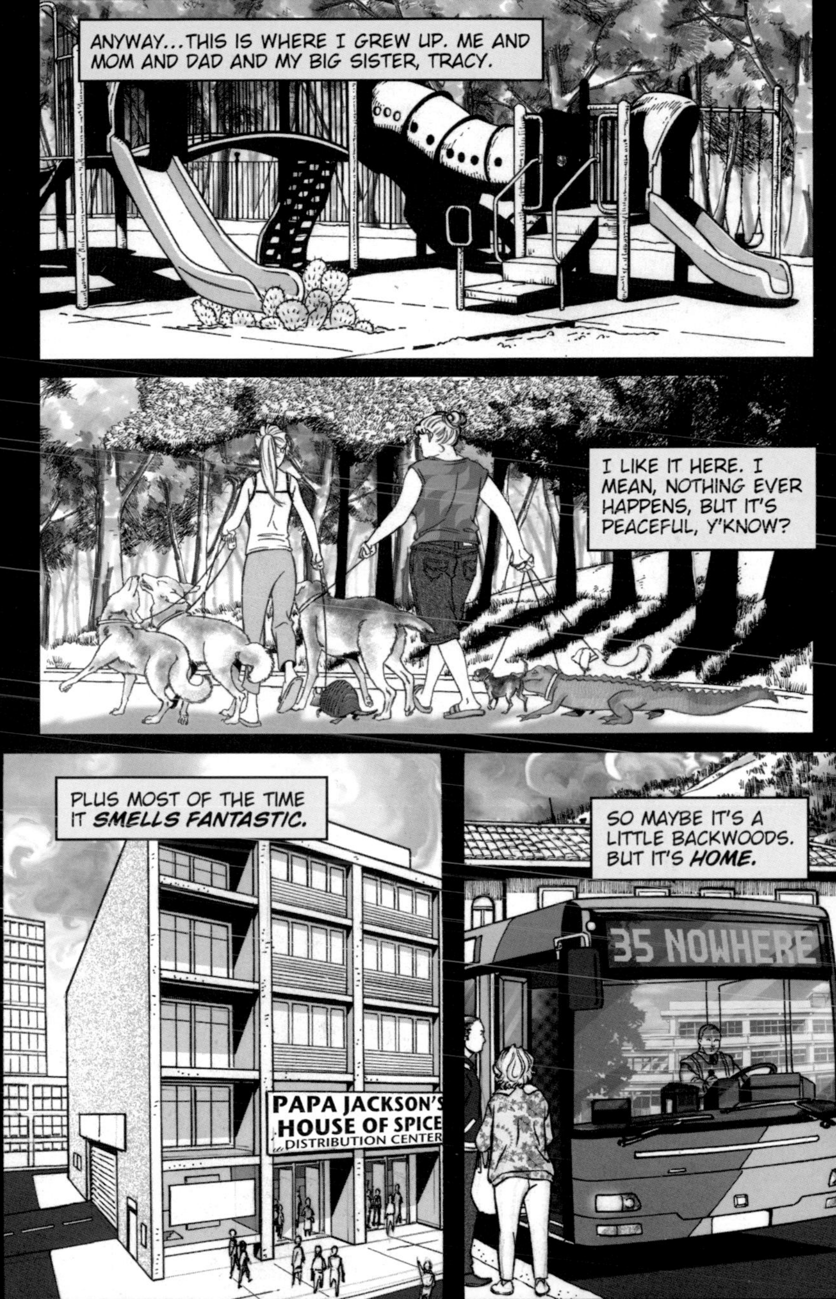
ANYWAY...THIS IS WHERE I GREW UP. ME AND MOM AND DAD AND MY BIG SISTER, TRACY.
I LIKE IT HERE. I MEAN, NOTHING EVER HAPPENS, BUT IT'S PEACEFUL, Y'KNOW?
PLUS MOST OF THE TIME IT SMELLS FANTASTIC.
PAPA JACKSON'S HOUSE OF SPICE DISTRIBUTION CENTER
SO MAYBE IT'S A LITTLE BACKWOODS. BUT IT'S HOME.
35 NOWHERE

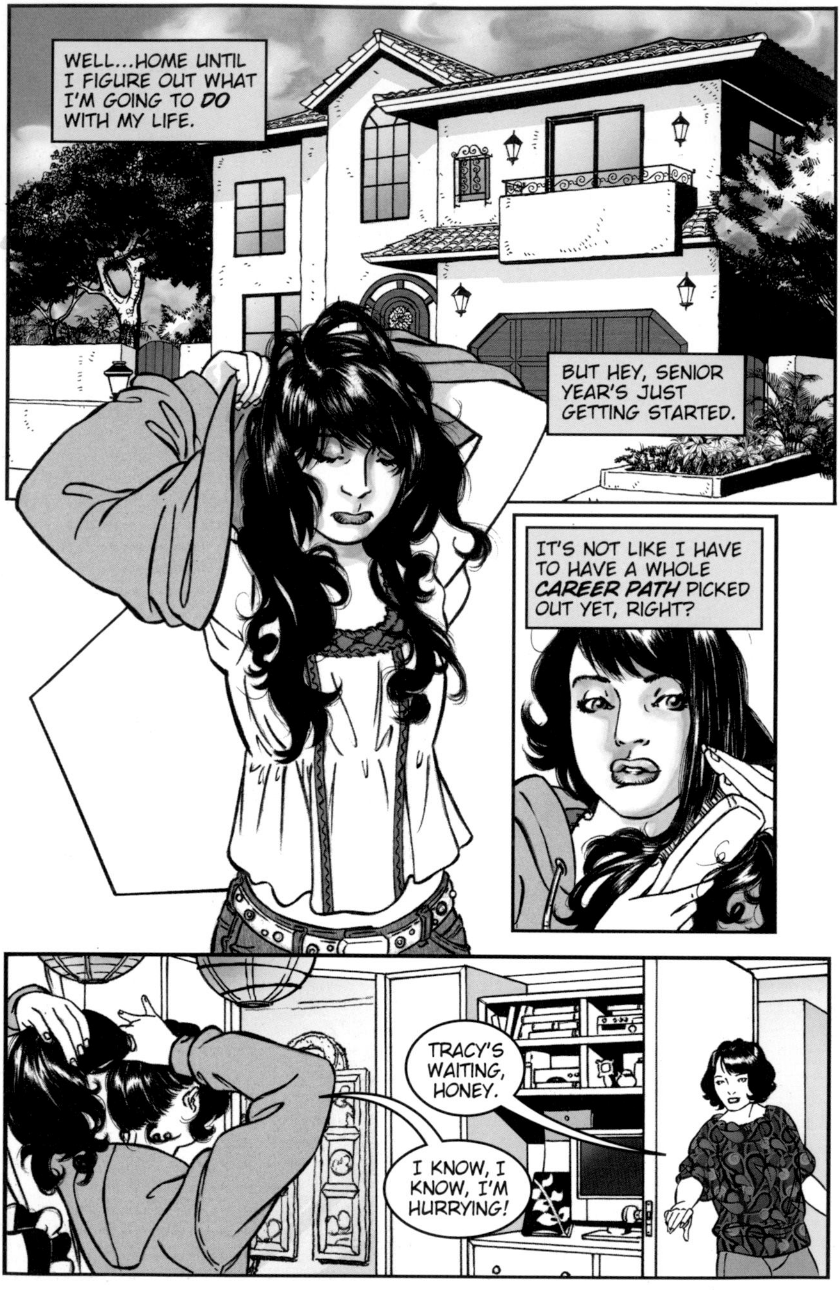
WELL...HOME UNTIL I FIGURE OUT WHAT I'M GOING TO ***DO*** WITH MY LIFE.
BUT HEY, SENIOR YEAR'S JUST GETTING STARTED.
IT'S NOT LIKE I HAVE TO HAVE A WHOLE ***CAREER PATH*** PICKED OUT YET, RIGHT?
TRACY'S WAITING, HONEY.
I KNOW, I KNOW, I'M HURRYING!

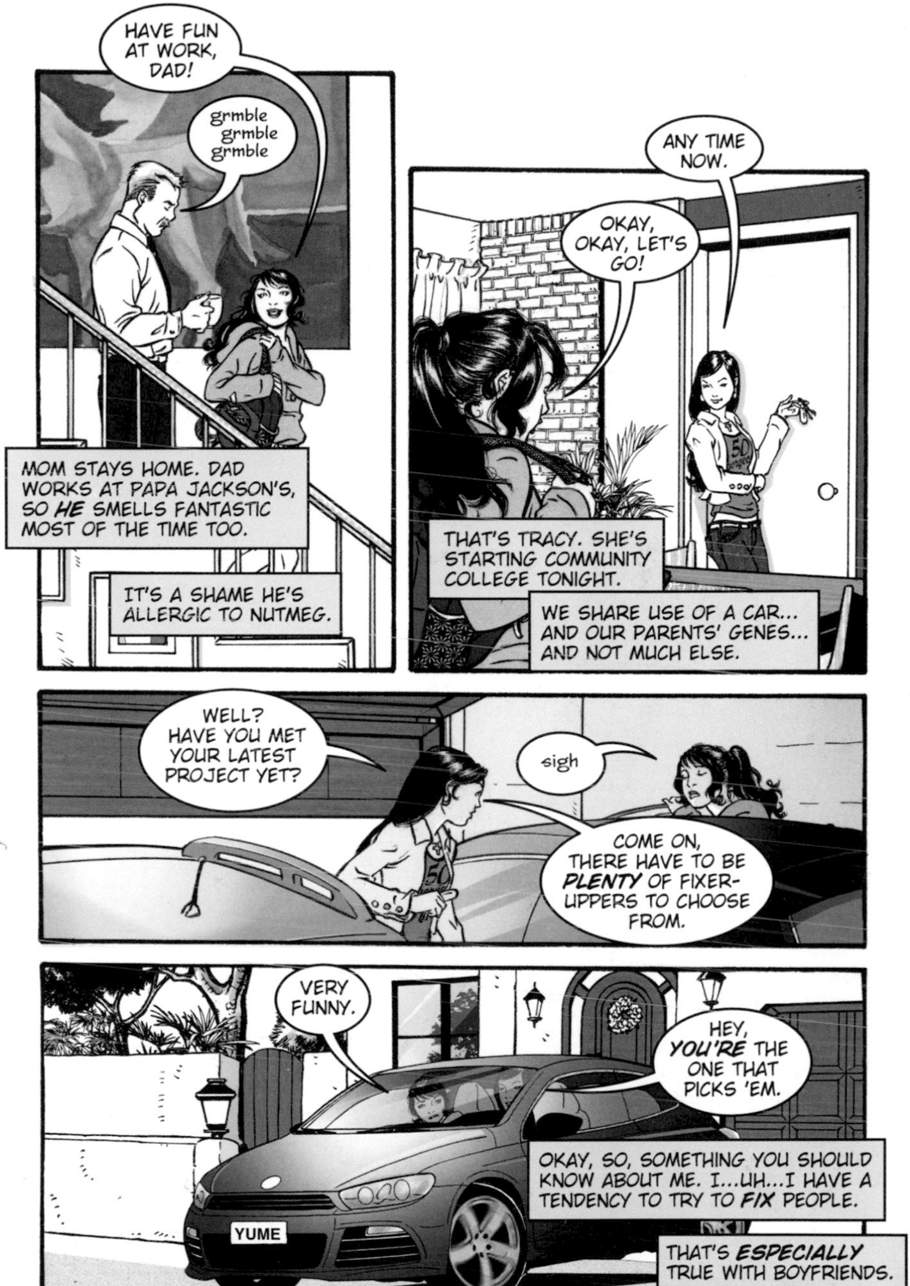

HAVE FUN AT WORK, DAD!
grmble grmble grmble
MOM STAYS HOME. DAD WORKS AT PAPA JACKSON'S, SO **HE** SMELLS FANTASTIC MOST OF THE TIME TOO.
IT'S A SHAME HE'S ALLERGIC TO NUTMEG.
ANY TIME NOW.
OKAY, OKAY, LET'S GO!
THAT'S TRACY. SHE'S STARTING COMMUNITY COLLEGE TONIGHT.
WE SHARE USE OF A CAR... AND OUR PARENTS' GENES... AND NOT MUCH ELSE.
WELL? HAVE YOU MET YOUR LATEST PROJECT YET?
sigh
COME ON, THERE HAVE TO BE **PLENTY** OF FIXER-UPPERS TO CHOOSE FROM.
VERY FUNNY.
HEY, **YOU'RE** THE ONE THAT PICKS 'EM.
YUME
OKAY, SO, SOMETHING YOU SHOULD KNOW ABOUT ME. I...UH...I HAVE A TENDENCY TO TRY TO **FIX** PEOPLE.
THAT'S **ESPECIALLY** TRUE WITH BOYFRIENDS.

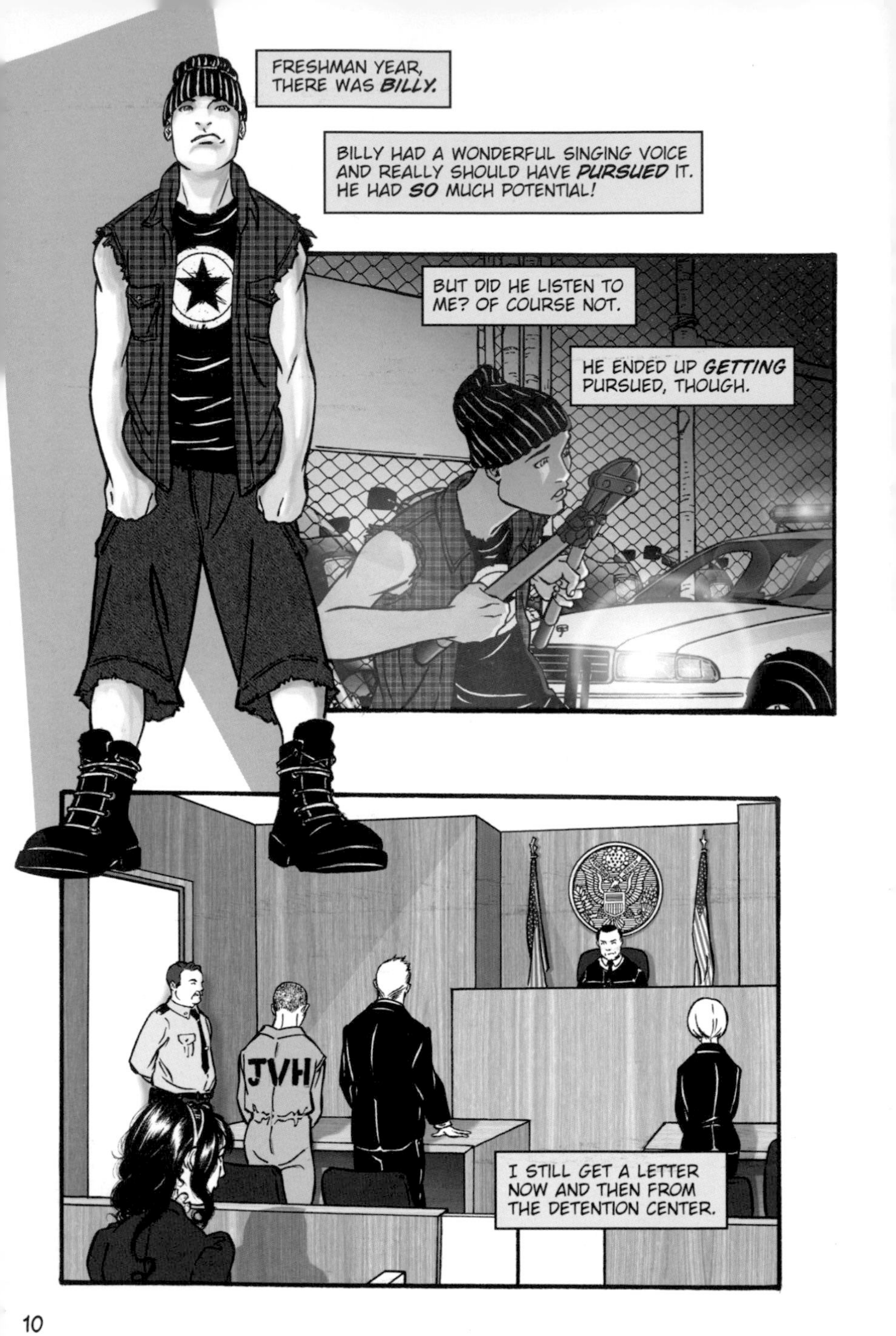
FRESHMAN YEAR, THERE WAS BILLY.
BILLY HAD A WONDERFUL SINGING VOICE AND REALLY SHOULD HAVE PURSUED IT. HE HAD SO MUCH POTENTIAL!
BUT DID HE LISTEN TO ME? OF COURSE NOT.
HE ENDED UP GETTING PURSUED, THOUGH.
JVH
I STILL GET A LETTER NOW AND THEN FROM THE DETENTION CENTER.

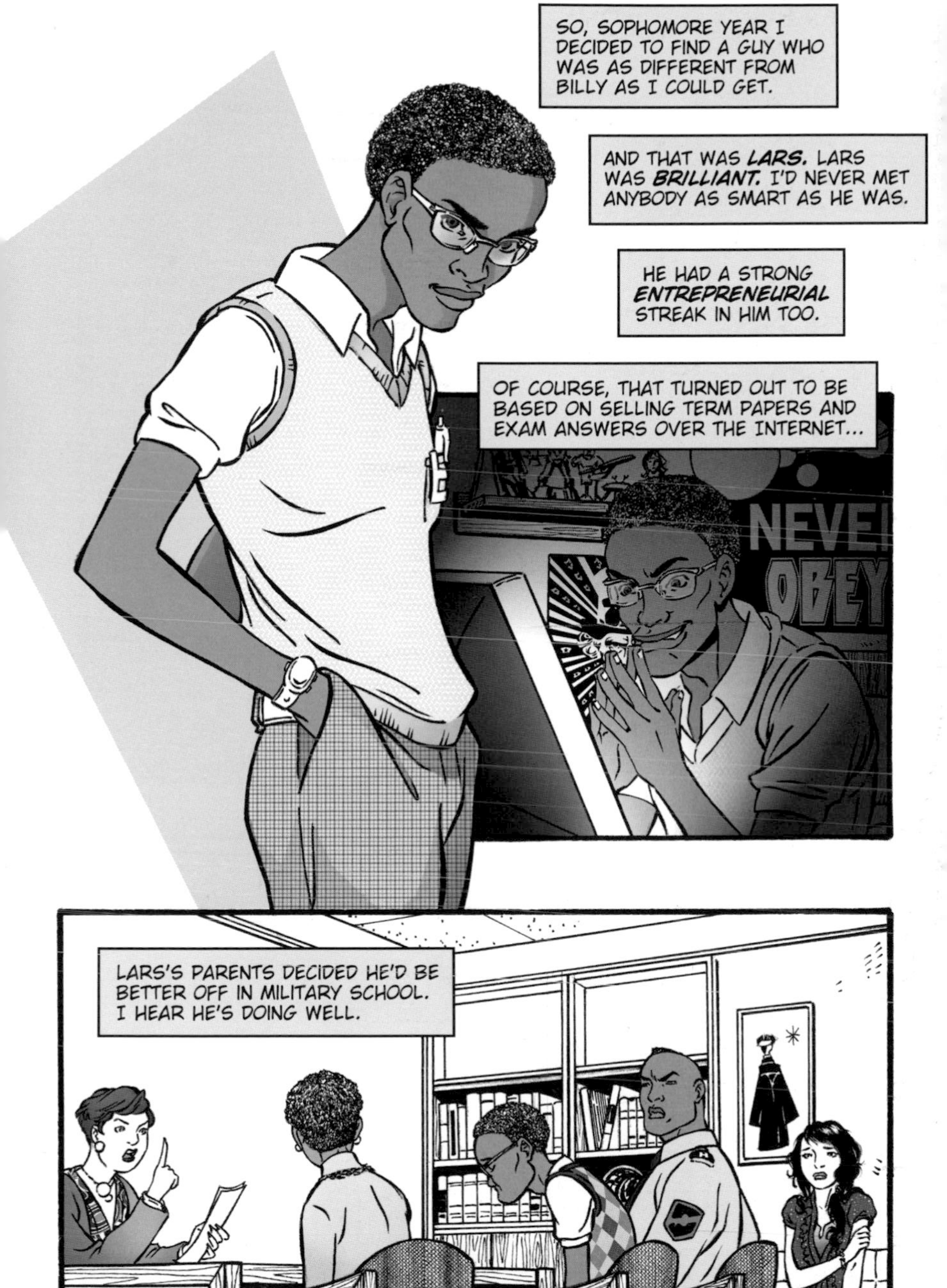
SO, SOPHOMORE YEAR I DECIDED TO FIND A GUY WHO WAS AS DIFFERENT FROM BILLY AS I COULD GET.
AND THAT WAS LARS. LARS WAS BRILLIANT. I'D NEVER MET ANYBODY AS SMART AS HE WAS.
HE HAD A STRONG ENTREPRENEURIAL STREAK IN HIM TOO.
OF COURSE, THAT TURNED OUT TO BE BASED ON SELLING TERM PAPERS AND EXAM ANSWERS OVER THE INTERNET...
NEVE
OBEY
LARS'S PARENTS DECIDED HE'D BE BETTER OFF IN MILITARY SCHOOL. I HEAR HE'S DOING WELL.

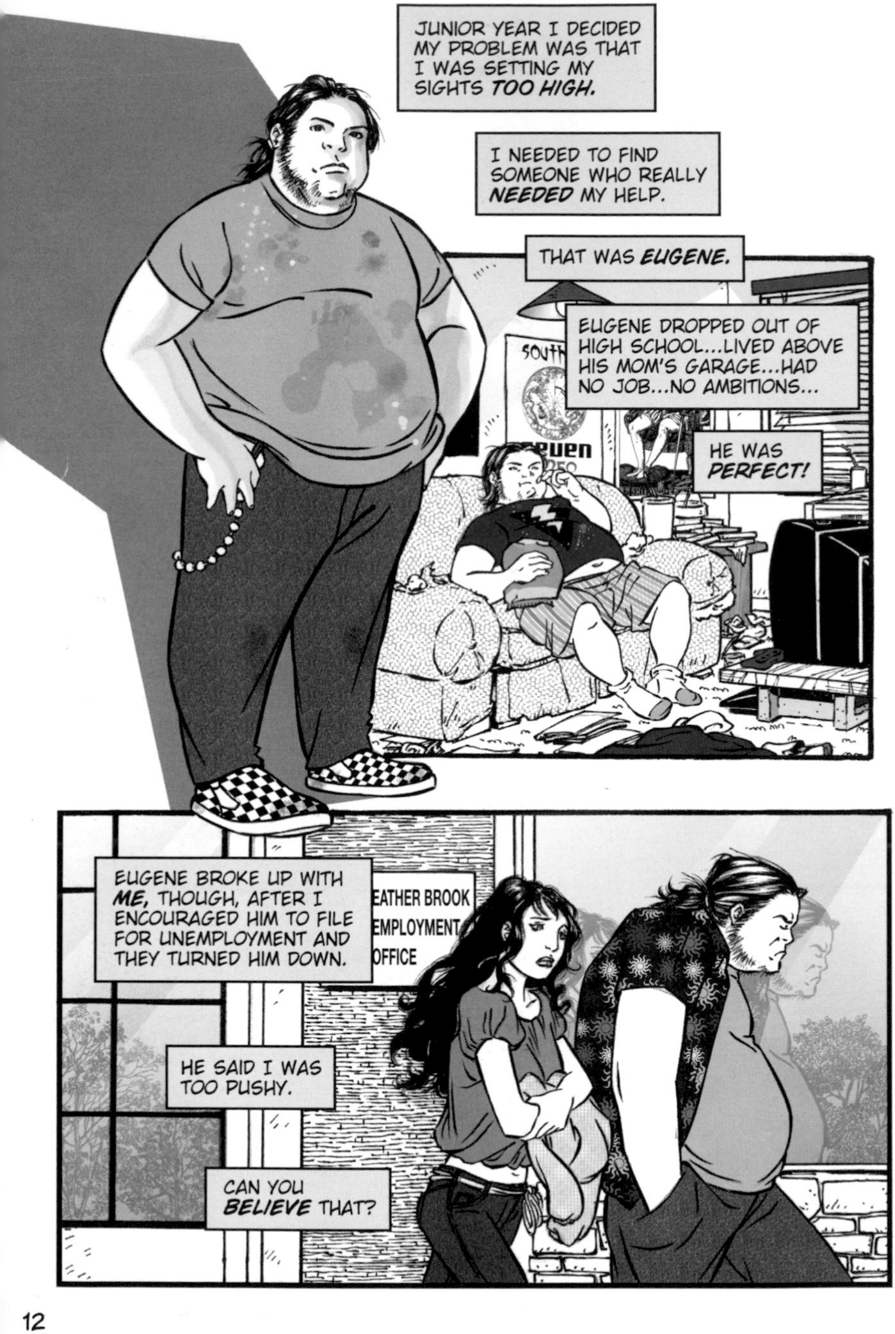
JUNIOR YEAR I DECIDED MY PROBLEM WAS THAT I WAS SETTING MY SIGHTS TOO HIGH.
I NEEDED TO FIND SOMEONE WHO REALLY NEEDED MY HELP.
THAT WAS EUGENE.
EUGENE DROPPED OUT OF HIGH SCHOOL...LIVED ABOVE HIS MOM'S GARAGE...HAD NO JOB...NO AMBITIONS...
HE WAS PERFECT!
EUGENE BROKE UP WITH ME, THOUGH, AFTER I ENCOURAGED HIM TO FILE FOR UNEMPLOYMENT AND THEY TURNED HIM DOWN.
EATHER BROOK
EMPLOYMENT
OFFICE
HE SAID I WAS TOO PUSHY.
CAN YOU BELIEVE THAT?

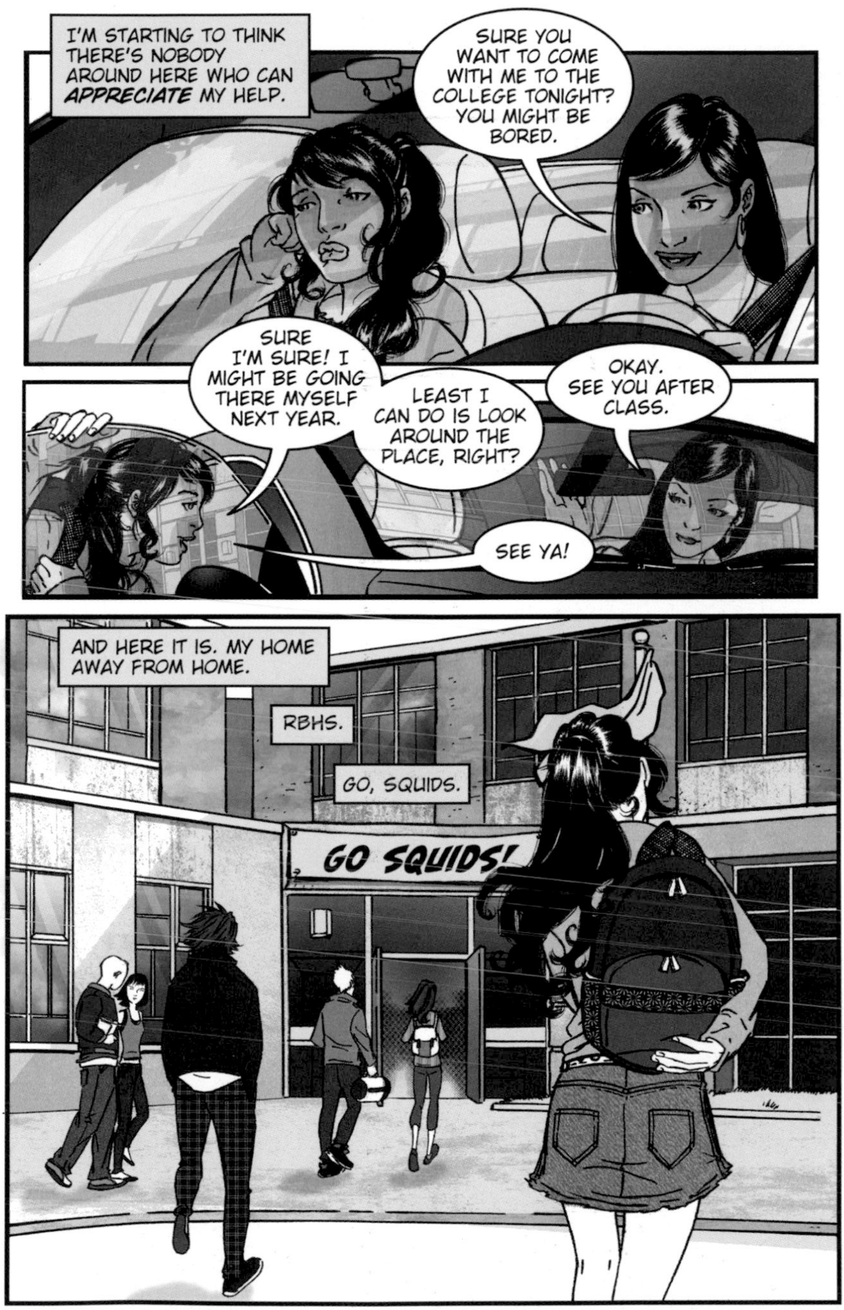
I'M STARTING TO THINK THERE'S NOBODY AROUND HERE WHO CAN *APPRECIATE* MY HELP.
SURE YOU WANT TO COME WITH ME TO THE COLLEGE TONIGHT? YOU MIGHT BE BORED.
SURE I'M SURE! I MIGHT BE GOING THERE MYSELF NEXT YEAR.
LEAST I CAN DO IS LOOK AROUND THE PLACE, RIGHT?
OKAY. SEE YOU AFTER CLASS.
SEE YA!
AND HERE IT IS. MY HOME AWAY FROM HOME.
RBHS.
GO, SQUIDS.
GO SQUIDS!

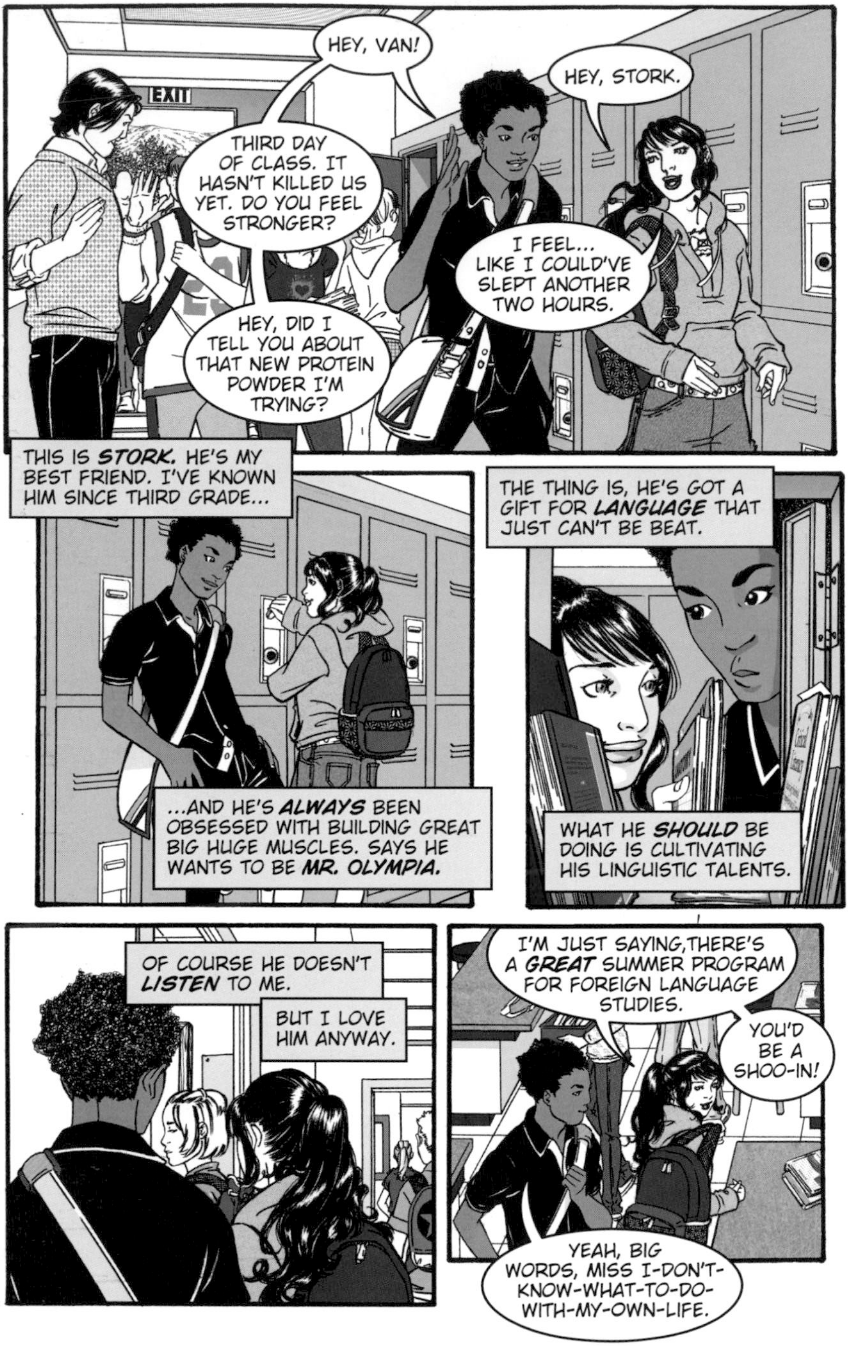
HEY, VAN!
HEY, STORK.
THIRD DAY OF CLASS. IT HASN'T KILLED US YET. DO YOU FEEL STRONGER?
I FEEL... LIKE I COULD'VE SLEPT ANOTHER TWO HOURS.
HEY, DID I TELL YOU ABOUT THAT NEW PROTEIN POWDER I'M TRYING?
EXIT
THIS IS **STORK.** HE'S MY BEST FRIEND. I'VE KNOWN HIM SINCE THIRD GRADE...
...AND HE'S **ALWAYS** BEEN OBSESSED WITH BUILDING GREAT BIG HUGE MUSCLES. SAYS HE WANTS TO BE **MR. OLYMPIA.**
THE THING IS, HE'S GOT A GIFT FOR **LANGUAGE** THAT JUST CAN'T BE BEAT.
WHAT HE **SHOULD** BE DOING IS CULTIVATING HIS LINGUISTIC TALENTS.
OF COURSE HE DOESN'T **LISTEN** TO ME.
BUT I LOVE HIM ANYWAY.
I'M JUST SAYING,THERE'S A **GREAT** SUMMER PROGRAM FOR FOREIGN LANGUAGE STUDIES.
YOU'D BE A SHOO-IN!
YEAH, BIG WORDS, MISS I-DON'T-KNOW-WHAT-TO-DO-WITH-MY-OWN-LIFE.

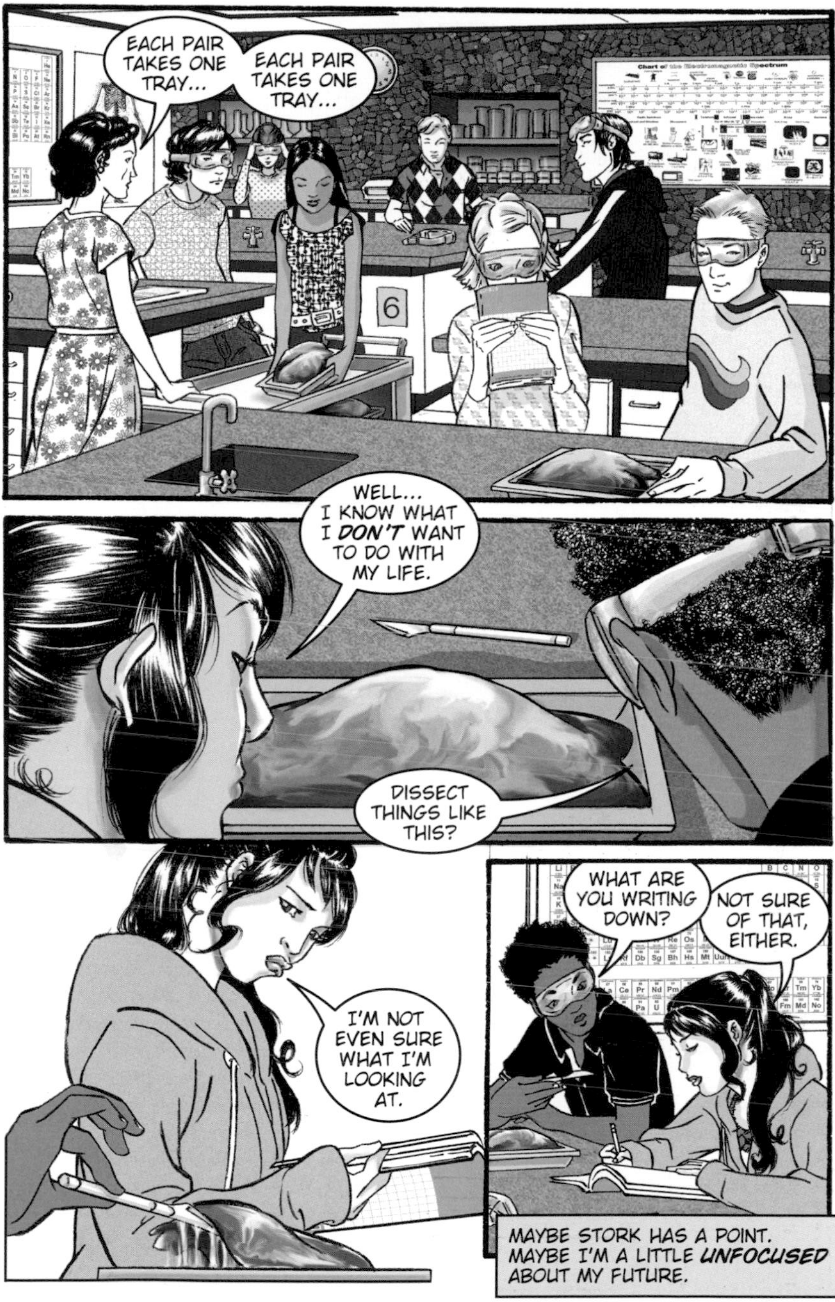
EACH PAIR TAKES ONE TRAY...
EACH PAIR TAKES ONE TRAY...
WELL... I KNOW WHAT I DON'T WANT TO DO WITH MY LIFE.
DISSECT THINGS LIKE THIS?
I'M NOT EVEN SURE WHAT I'M LOOKING AT.
WHAT ARE YOU WRITING DOWN?
NOT SURE OF THAT, EITHER.
MAYBE STORK HAS A POINT. MAYBE I'M A LITTLE UNFOCUSED ABOUT MY FUTURE.

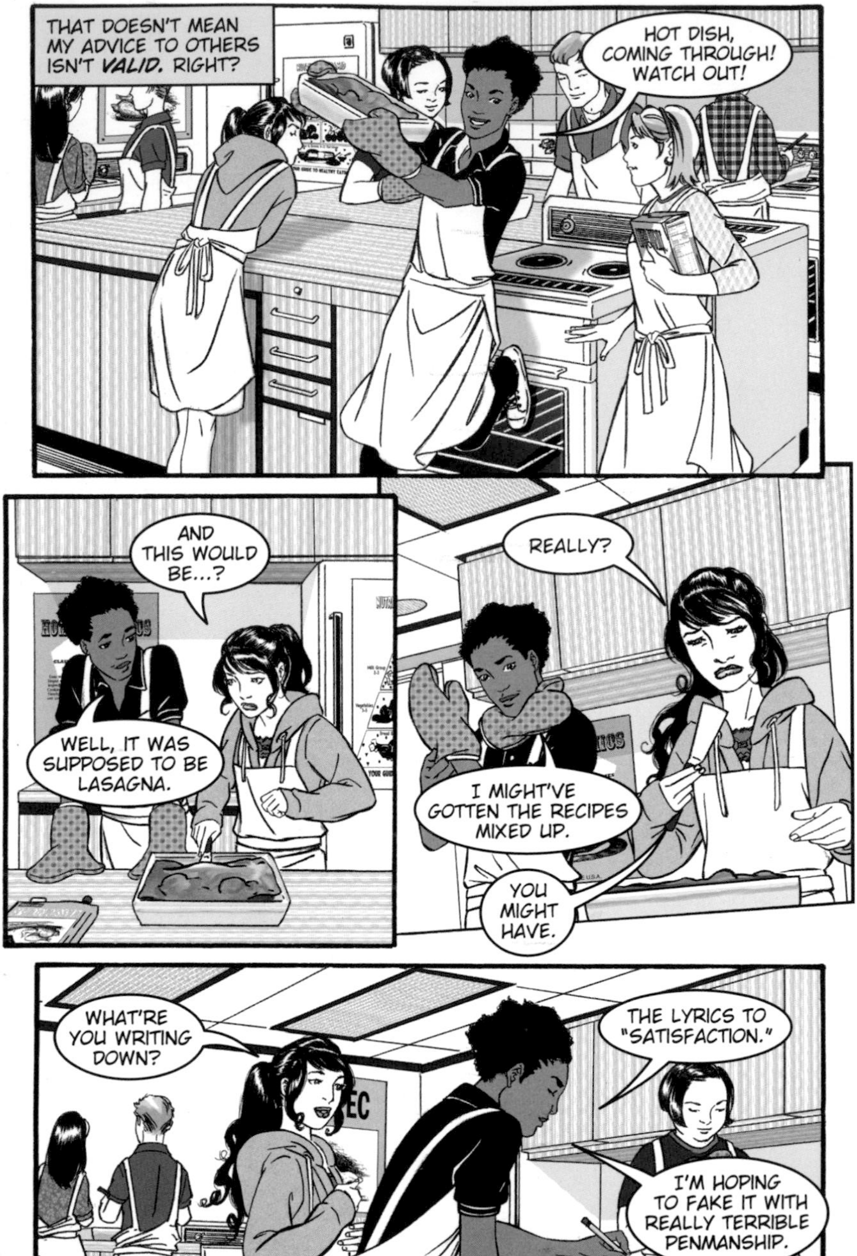
THAT DOESN'T MEAN MY ADVICE TO OTHERS ISN'T *VALID.* RIGHT?
HOT DISH, COMING THROUGH! WATCH OUT!
AND THIS WOULD BE...?
WELL, IT WAS SUPPOSED TO BE LASAGNA.
REALLY?
I MIGHT'VE GOTTEN THE RECIPES MIXED UP.
YOU MIGHT HAVE.
WHAT'RE YOU WRITING DOWN?
THE LYRICS TO "SATISFACTION."
I'M HOPING TO FAKE IT WITH REALLY TERRIBLE PENMANSHIP.

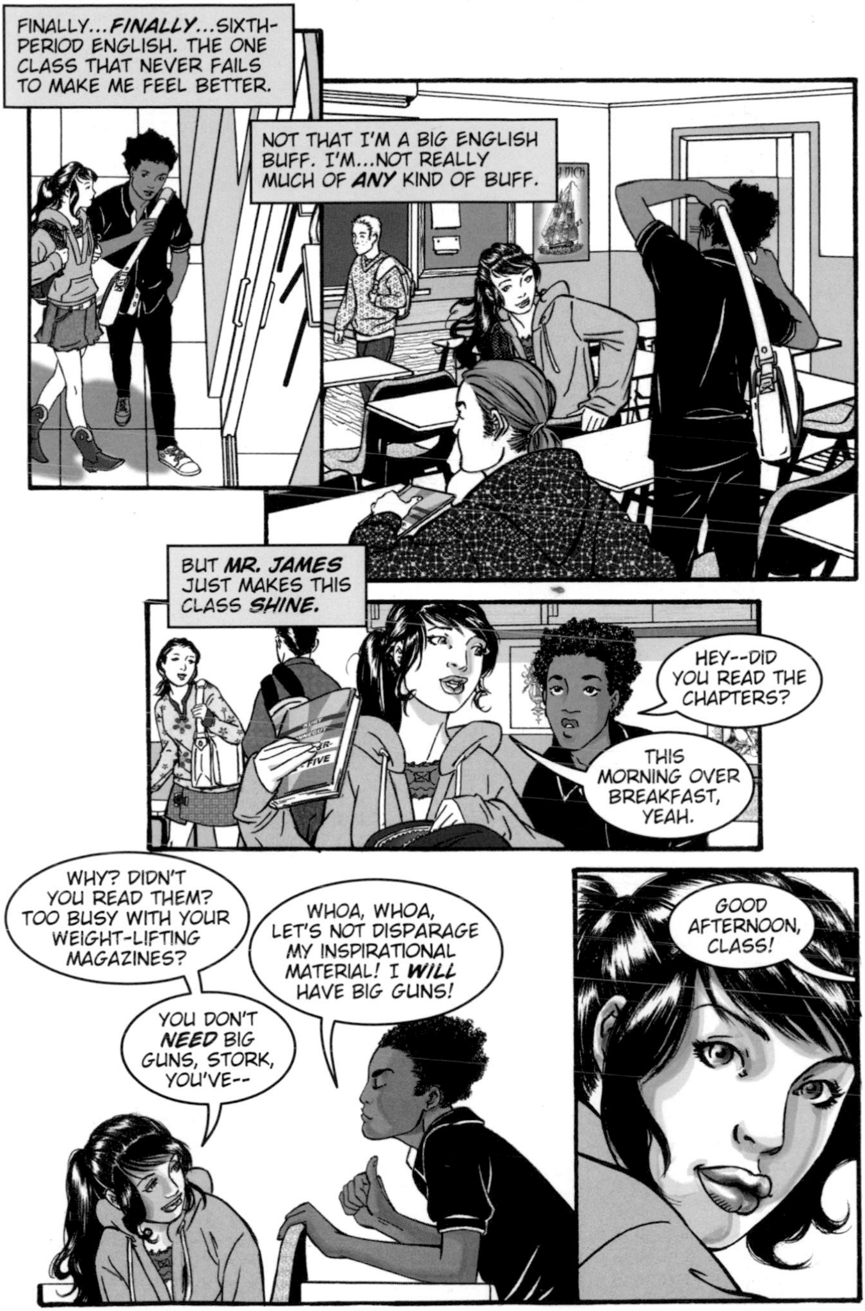
FINALLY...FINALLY...SIXTH-PERIOD ENGLISH. THE ONE CLASS THAT NEVER FAILS TO MAKE ME FEEL BETTER.
NOT THAT I'M A BIG ENGLISH BUFF. I'M...NOT REALLY MUCH OF ANY KIND OF BUFF.
BUT MR. JAMES JUST MAKES THIS CLASS SHINE.
HEY--DID YOU READ THE CHAPTERS?
THIS MORNING OVER BREAKFAST, YEAH.
WHY? DIDN'T YOU READ THEM? TOO BUSY WITH YOUR WEIGHT-LIFTING MAGAZINES?
WHOA, WHOA, LET'S NOT DISPARAGE MY INSPIRATIONAL MATERIAL! I WILL HAVE BIG GUNS!
YOU DON'T NEED BIG GUNS, STORK, YOU'VE--
GOOD AFTERNOON, CLASS!

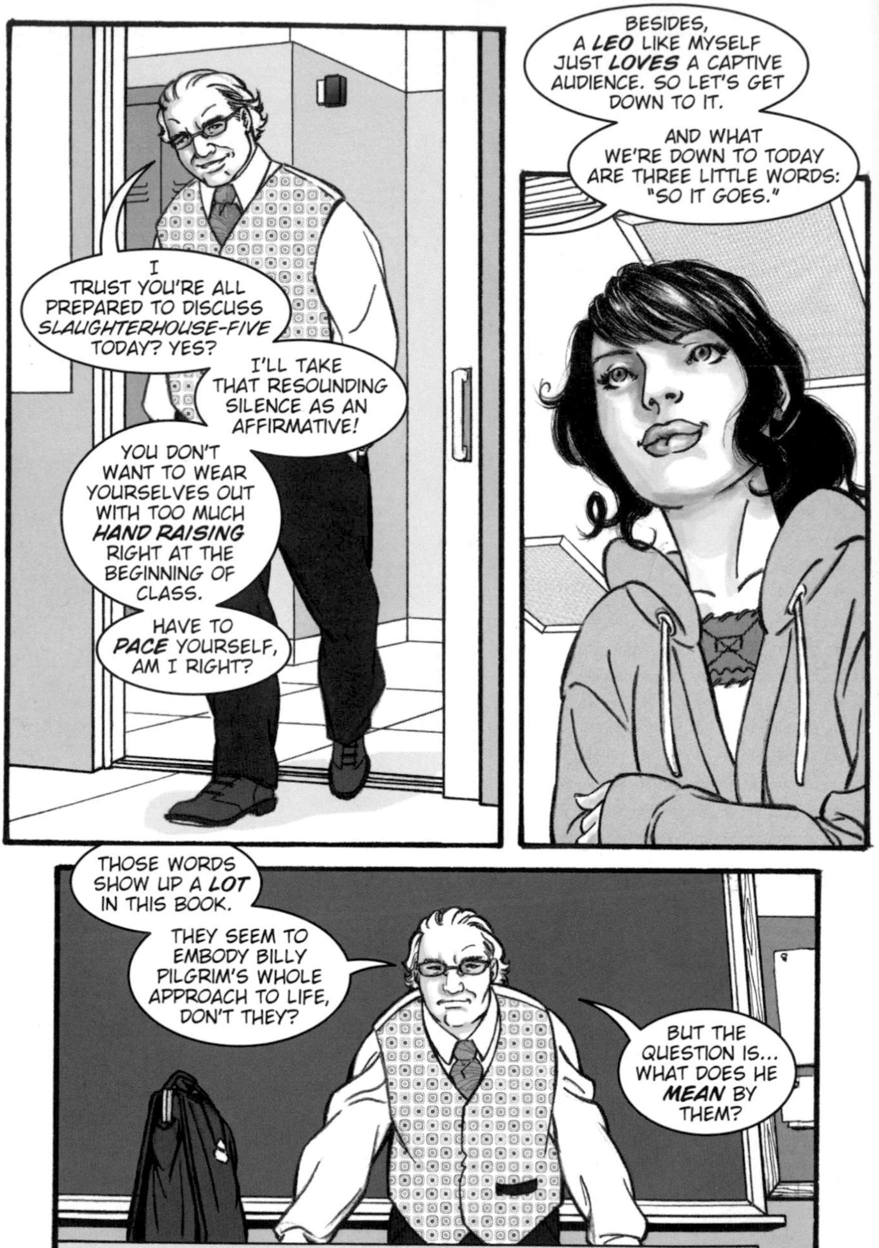
I TRUST YOU'RE ALL PREPARED TO DISCUSS *SLAUGHTERHOUSE-FIVE* TODAY? YES?
I'LL TAKE THAT RESOUNDING SILENCE AS AN AFFIRMATIVE!
YOU DON'T WANT TO WEAR YOURSELVES OUT WITH TOO MUCH **HAND RAISING** RIGHT AT THE BEGINNING OF CLASS.
HAVE TO **PACE** YOURSELF, AM I RIGHT?
BESIDES, A **LEO** LIKE MYSELF JUST **LOVES** A CAPTIVE AUDIENCE. SO LET'S GET DOWN TO IT.
AND WHAT WE'RE DOWN TO TODAY ARE THREE LITTLE WORDS: "SO IT GOES."
THOSE WORDS SHOW UP A **LOT** IN THIS BOOK.
THEY SEEM TO EMBODY BILLY PILGRIM'S WHOLE APPROACH TO LIFE, DON'T THEY?
BUT THE QUESTION IS... WHAT DOES HE **MEAN** BY THEM?

19

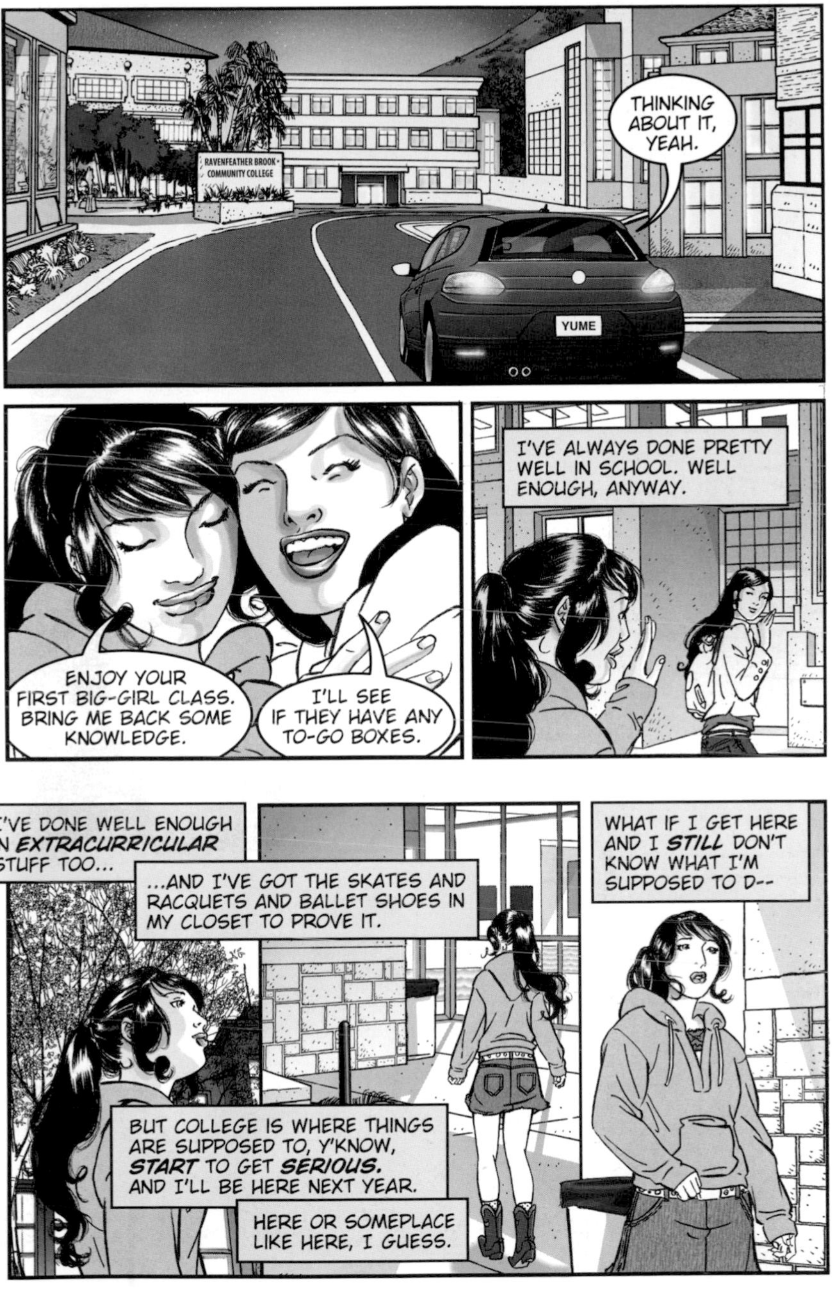
RAVENFEATHER BROOK COMMUNITY COLLEGE
THINKING ABOUT IT, YEAH.
YUME
ENJOY YOUR FIRST BIG-GIRL CLASS. BRING ME BACK SOME KNOWLEDGE.
I'LL SEE IF THEY HAVE ANY TO-GO BOXES.
I'VE ALWAYS DONE PRETTY WELL IN SCHOOL. WELL ENOUGH, ANYWAY.
I'VE DONE WELL ENOUGH IN EXTRACURRICULAR STUFF TOO...
...AND I'VE GOT THE SKATES AND RACQUETS AND BALLET SHOES IN MY CLOSET TO PROVE IT.
BUT COLLEGE IS WHERE THINGS ARE SUPPOSED TO, Y'KNOW, START TO GET SERIOUS. AND I'LL BE HERE NEXT YEAR.
HERE OR SOMEPLACE LIKE HERE, I GUESS.
WHAT IF I GET HERE AND I STILL DON'T KNOW WHAT I'M SUPPOSED TO D--

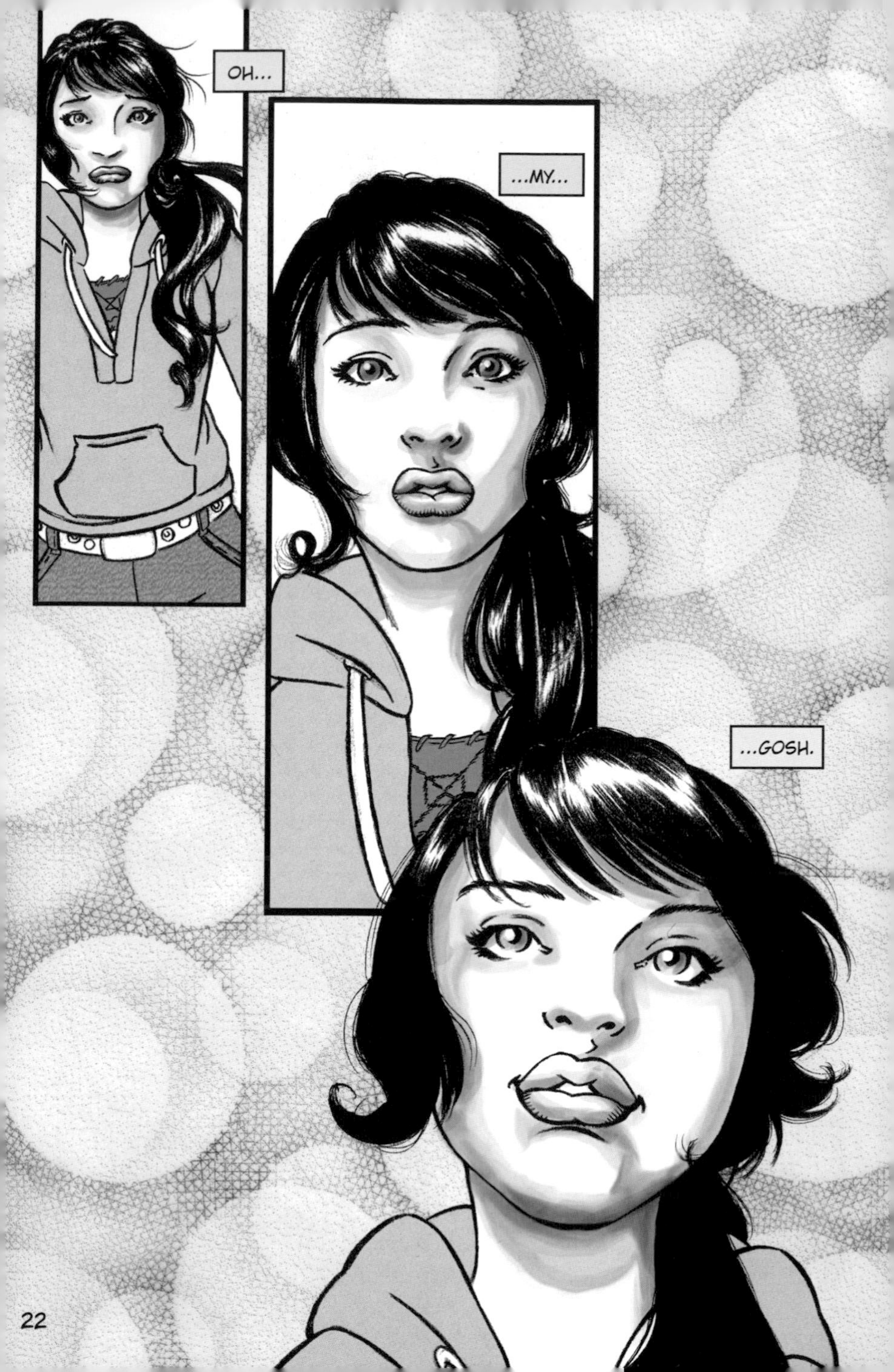
OH...
...MY...
...GOSH.

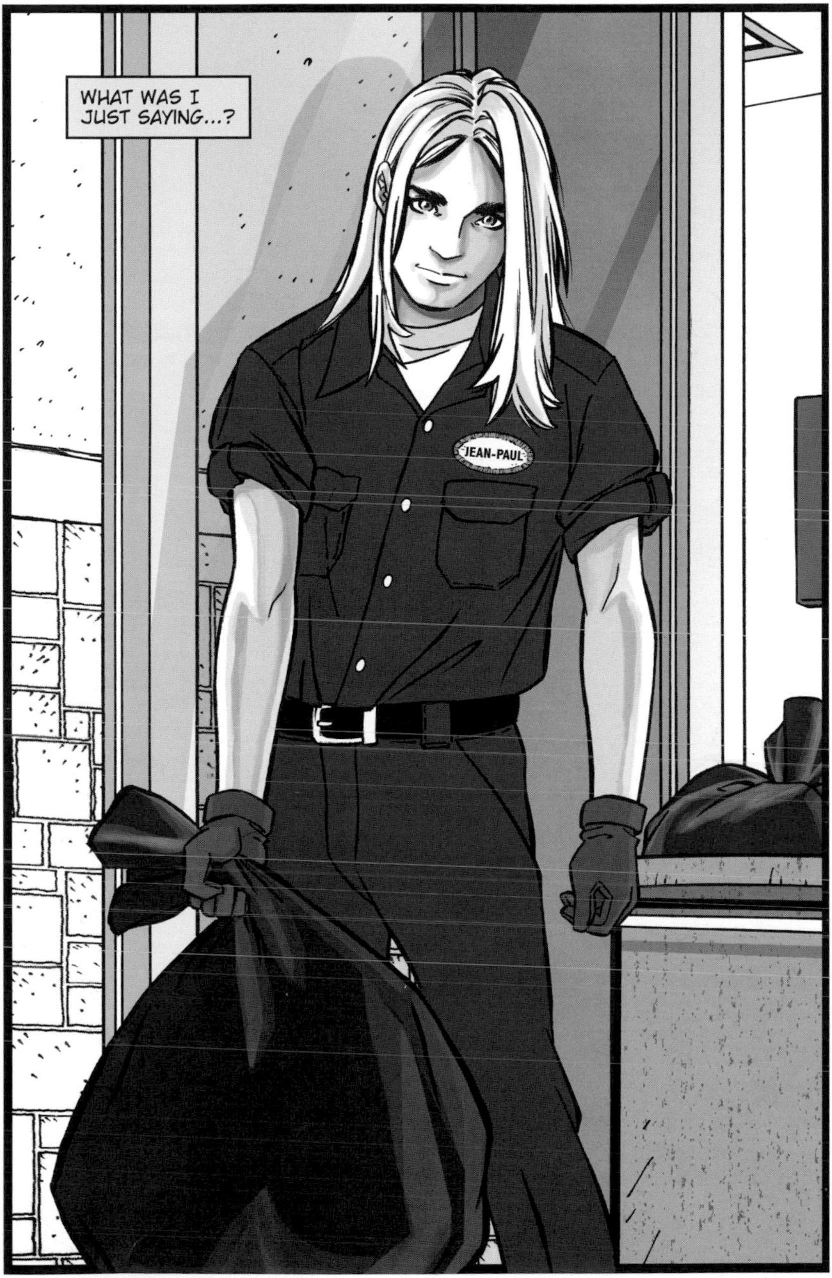
WHAT WAS I JUST SAYING...?
JEAN-PAUL

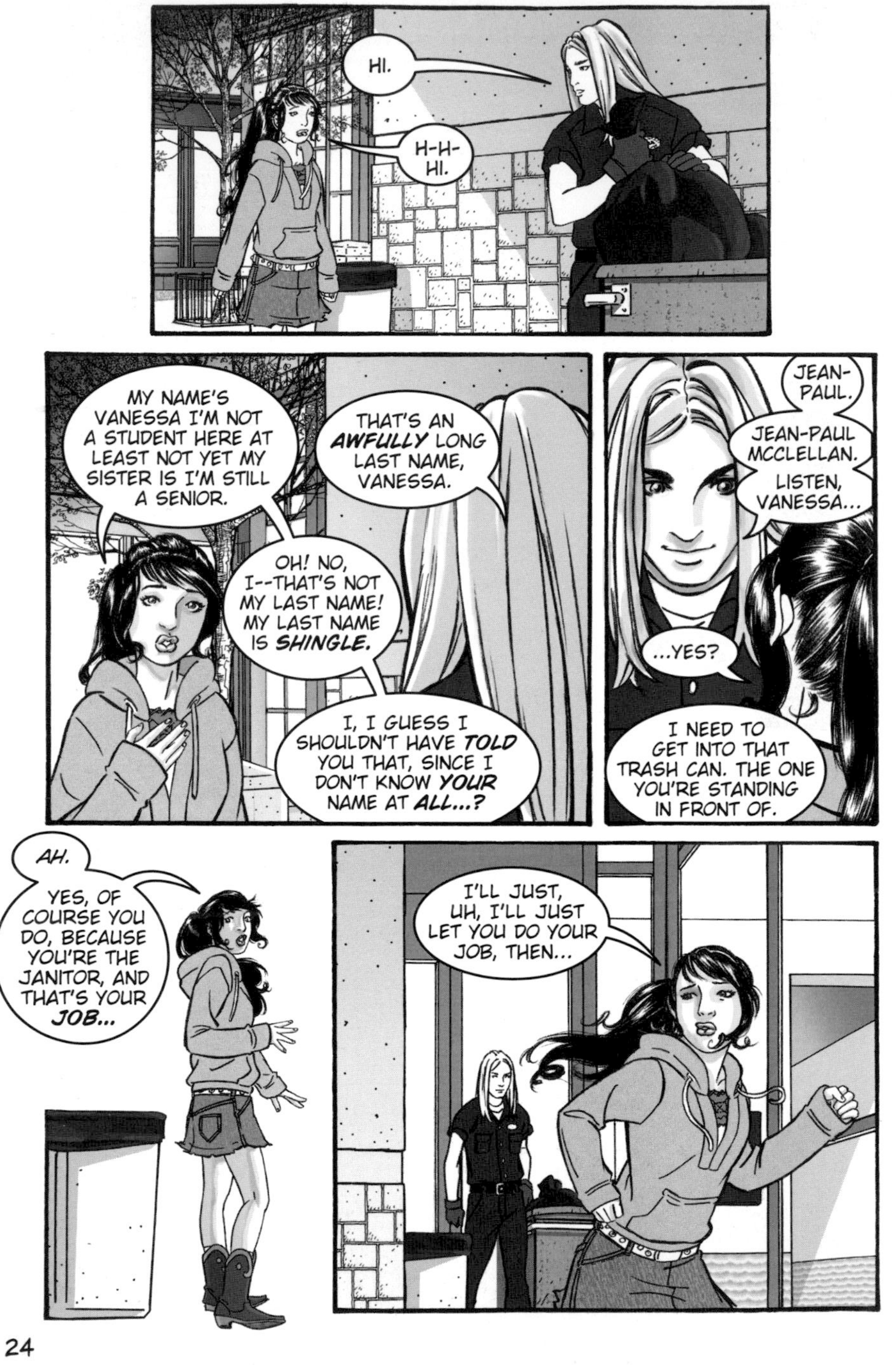
HI.
H-H-HI.
MY NAME'S VANESSA I'M NOT A STUDENT HERE AT LEAST NOT YET MY SISTER IS I'M STILL A SENIOR.
THAT'S AN *AWFULLY* LONG LAST NAME, VANESSA.
OH! NO, I--THAT'S NOT MY LAST NAME! MY LAST NAME IS *SHINGLE.*
I, I GUESS I SHOULDN'T HAVE *TOLD* YOU THAT, SINCE I DON'T KNOW *YOUR* NAME AT *ALL...?*
JEAN-PAUL.
JEAN-PAUL MCCLELLAN.
LISTEN, VANESSA...
...YES?
I NEED TO GET INTO THAT TRASH CAN. THE ONE YOU'RE STANDING IN FRONT OF.
AH.
YES, OF COURSE YOU DO, BECAUSE YOU'RE THE JANITOR, AND THAT'S YOUR *JOB...*
I'LL JUST, UH, I'LL JUST LET YOU DO YOUR JOB, THEN...

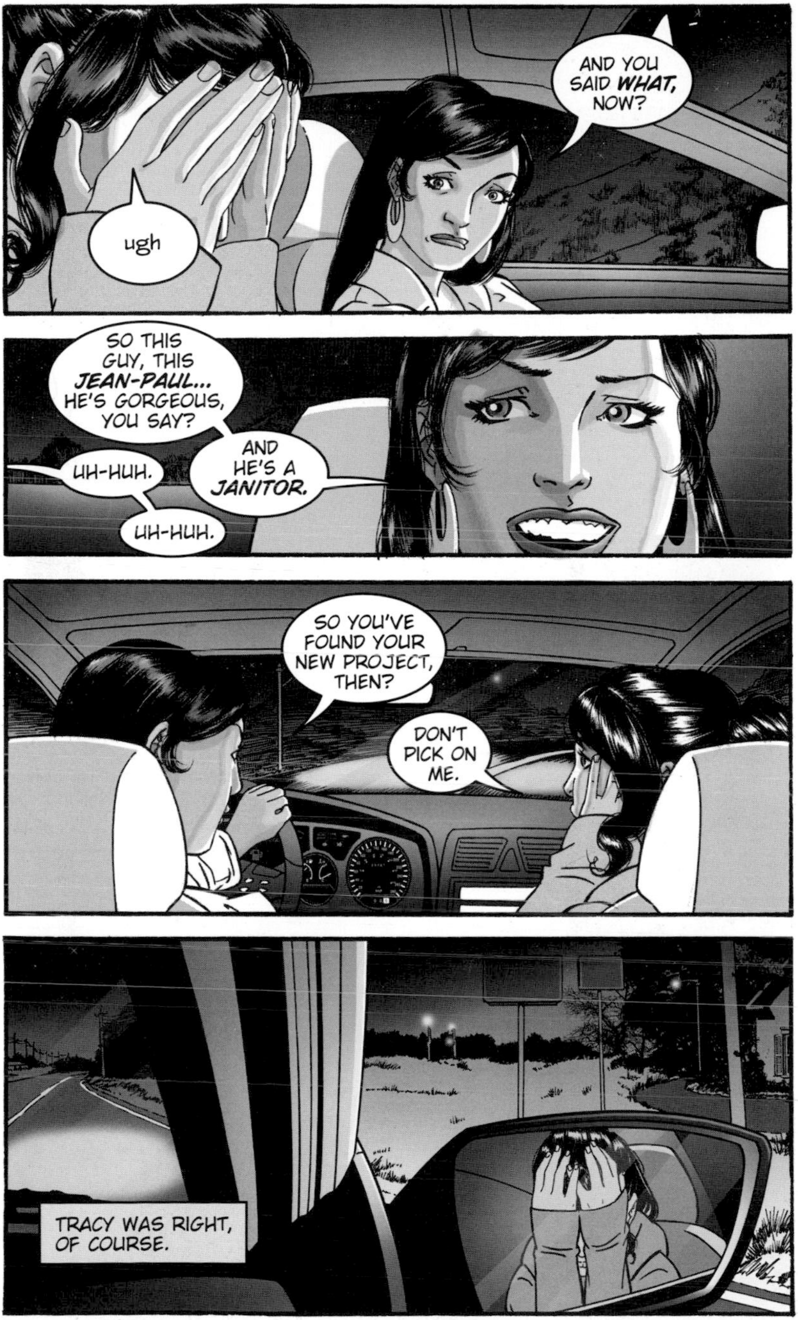

AND YOU SAID **WHAT,** NOW?
ugh
SO THIS GUY, THIS **JEAN-PAUL...** HE'S GORGEOUS, YOU SAY?
UH-HUH.
AND HE'S A **JANITOR.**
UH-HUH.
SO YOU'VE FOUND YOUR NEW PROJECT, THEN?
DON'T PICK ON ME.
TRACY WAS RIGHT, OF COURSE.

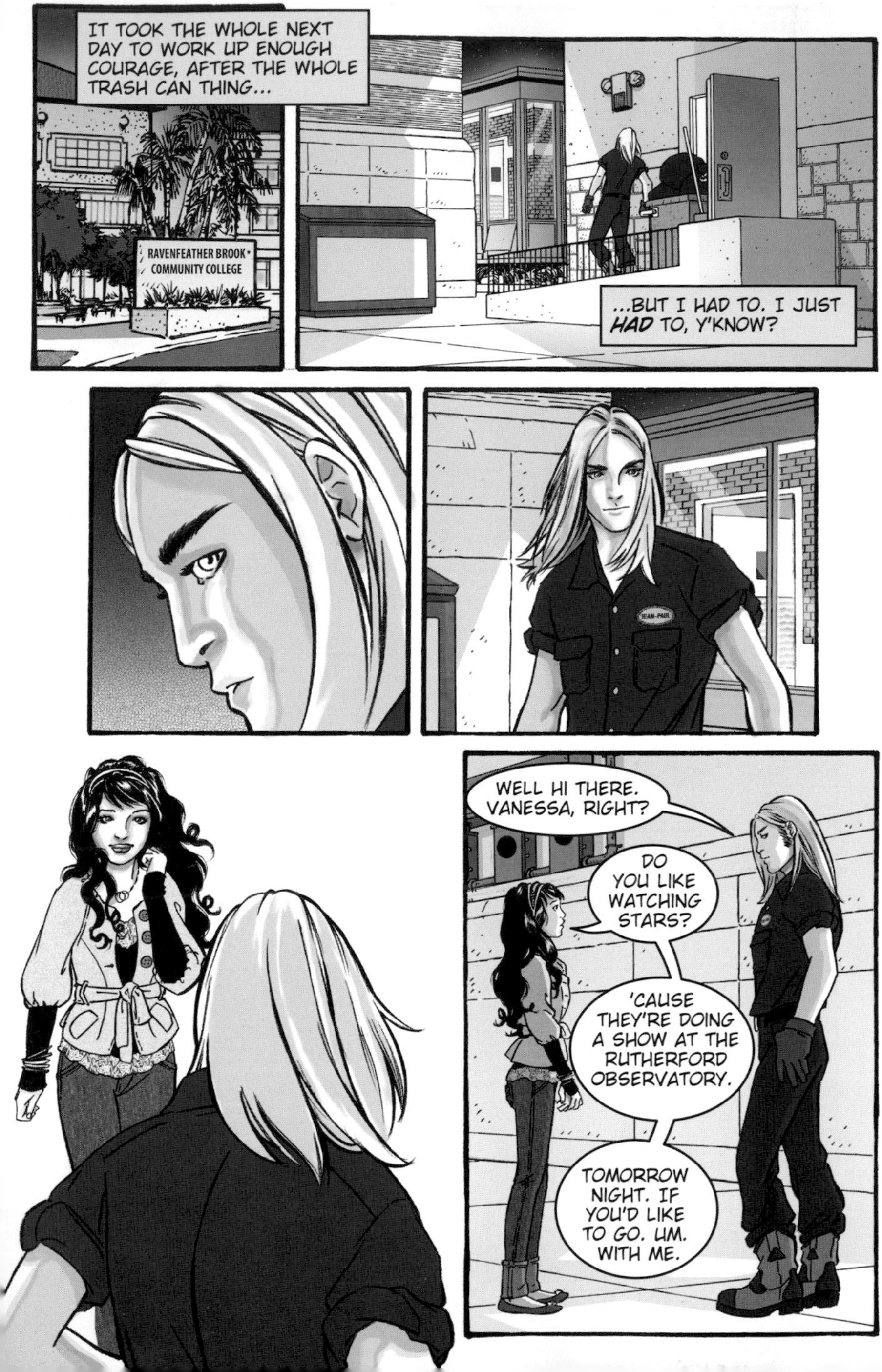
IT TOOK THE WHOLE NEXT DAY TO WORK UP ENOUGH COURAGE, AFTER THE WHOLE TRASH CAN THING...
RAVENFEATHER BROOK COMMUNITY COLLEGE
...BUT I HAD TO. I JUST HAD TO, Y'KNOW?
JEAN-PAUL
WELL HI THERE. VANESSA, RIGHT?
DO YOU LIKE WATCHING STARS?
'CAUSE THEY'RE DOING A SHOW AT THE RUTHERFORD OBSERVATORY.
TOMORROW NIGHT. IF YOU'D LIKE TO GO. UM. WITH ME.

27

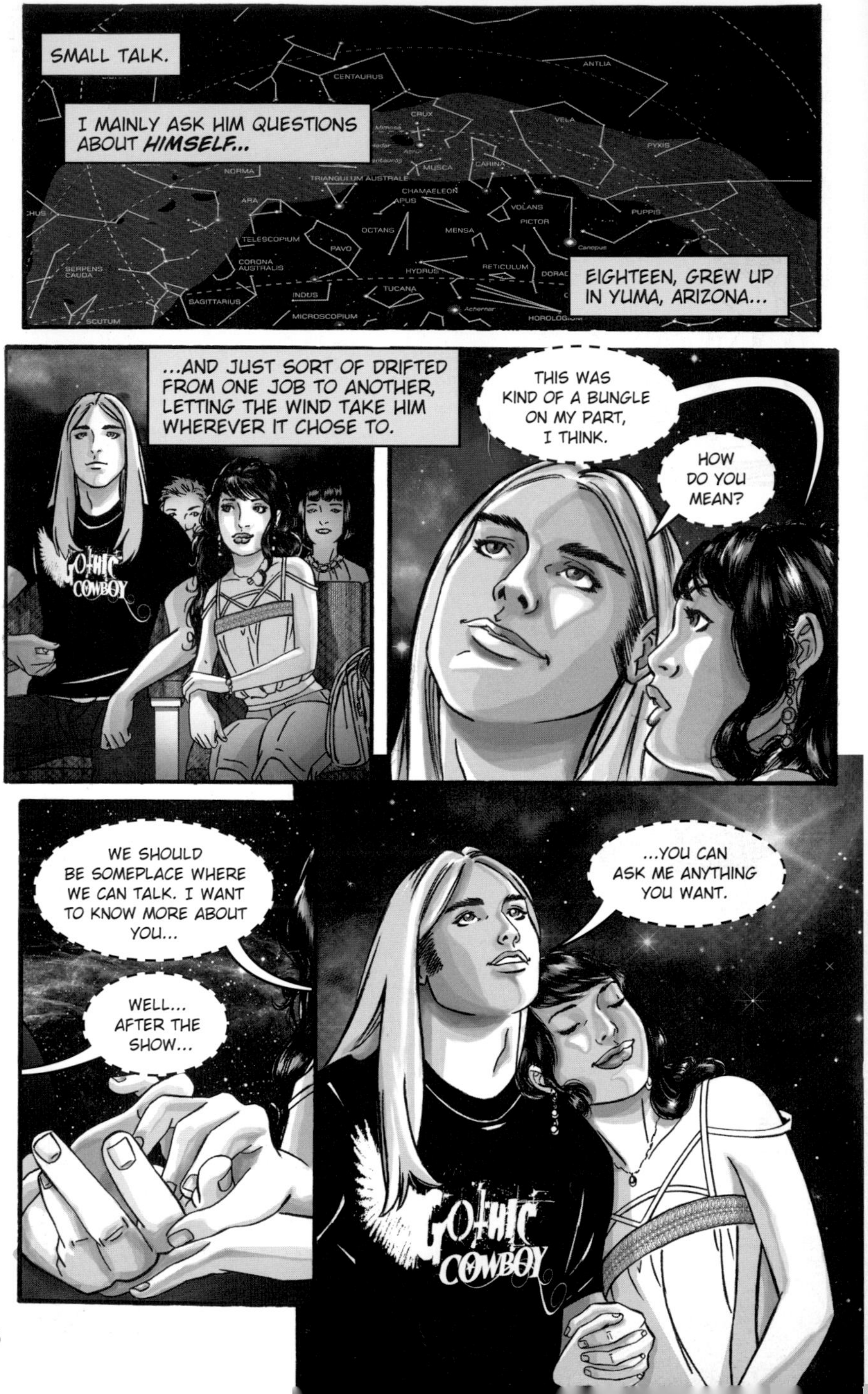
SMALL TALK.
I MAINLY ASK HIM QUESTIONS ABOUT *HIMSELF*...
CENTAURUS
ANTLIA
CRUX
VELA
PYXIS
NORMA
MUSCA
CARINA
TRIANGULUM AUSTRALE
CHAMAELEON
APUS
ARA
VOLANS
PICTOR
PUPPIS
TELESCOPIUM
OCTANS
MENSA
PAVO
Canopus
SERPENS CAUDA
CORONA AUSTRALIS
HYDRUS
RETICULUM
TUCANA
INDUS
SAGITTARIUS
MICROSCOPIUM
Achernar
SCUTUM
EIGHTEEN, GREW UP IN YUMA, ARIZONA...
...AND JUST SORT OF DRIFTED FROM ONE JOB TO ANOTHER, LETTING THE WIND TAKE HIM WHEREVER IT CHOSE TO.
GOTHIC COWBOY
THIS WAS KIND OF A BUNGLE ON MY PART, I THINK.
HOW DO YOU MEAN?
WE SHOULD BE SOMEPLACE WHERE WE CAN TALK. I WANT TO KNOW MORE ABOUT YOU...
WELL... AFTER THE SHOW...
...YOU CAN ASK ME ANYTHING YOU WANT.
GOTHIC COWBOY

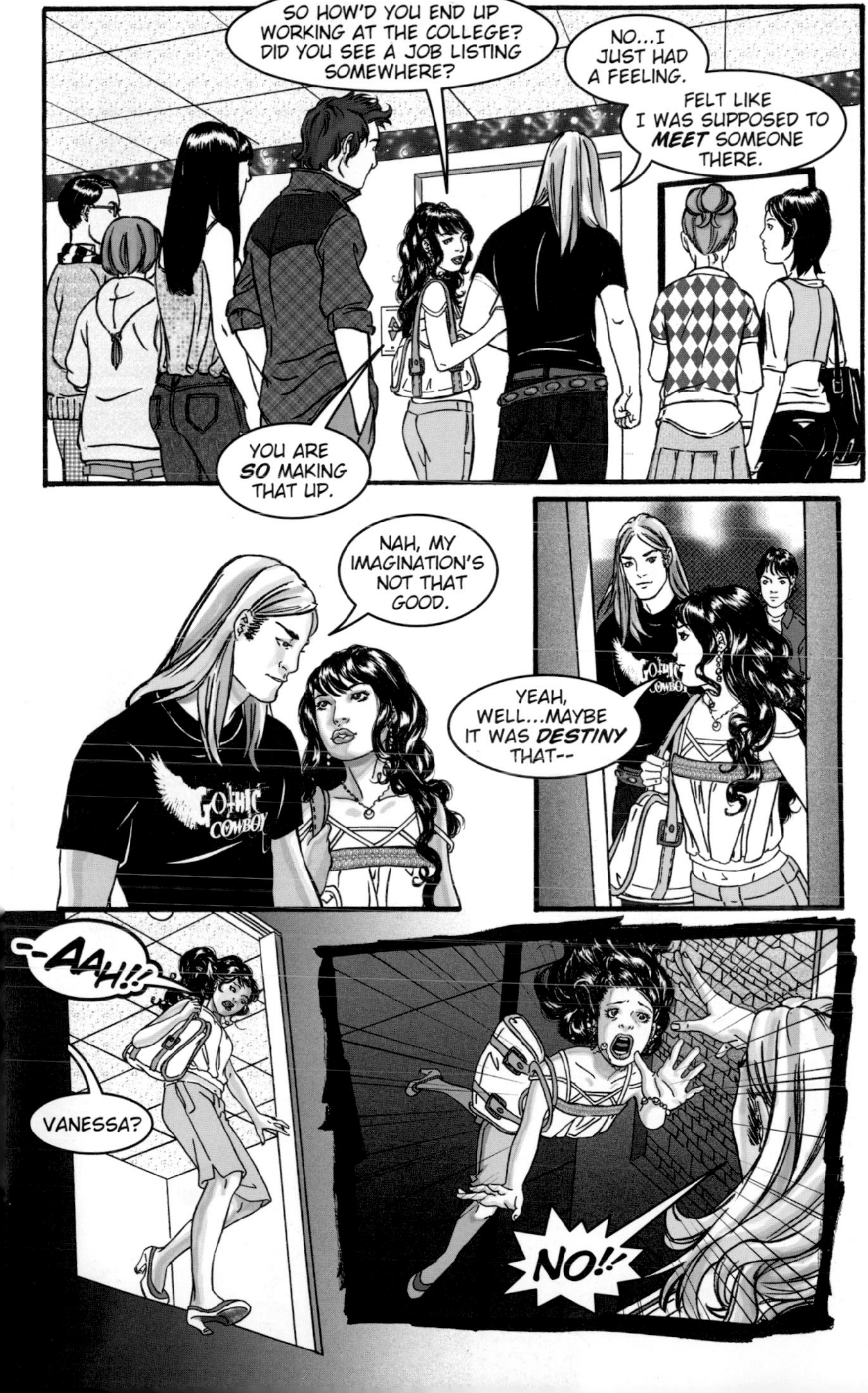
SO HOW'D YOU END UP WORKING AT THE COLLEGE? DID YOU SEE A JOB LISTING SOMEWHERE?
NO...I JUST HAD A FEELING.
FELT LIKE I WAS SUPPOSED TO *MEET* SOMEONE THERE.
YOU ARE *SO* MAKING THAT UP.
NAH, MY IMAGINATION'S NOT THAT GOOD.
GOTHIC COWBOY
YEAH, WELL...MAYBE IT WAS *DESTINY* THAT--
--AAH!!
VANESSA?
NO!!

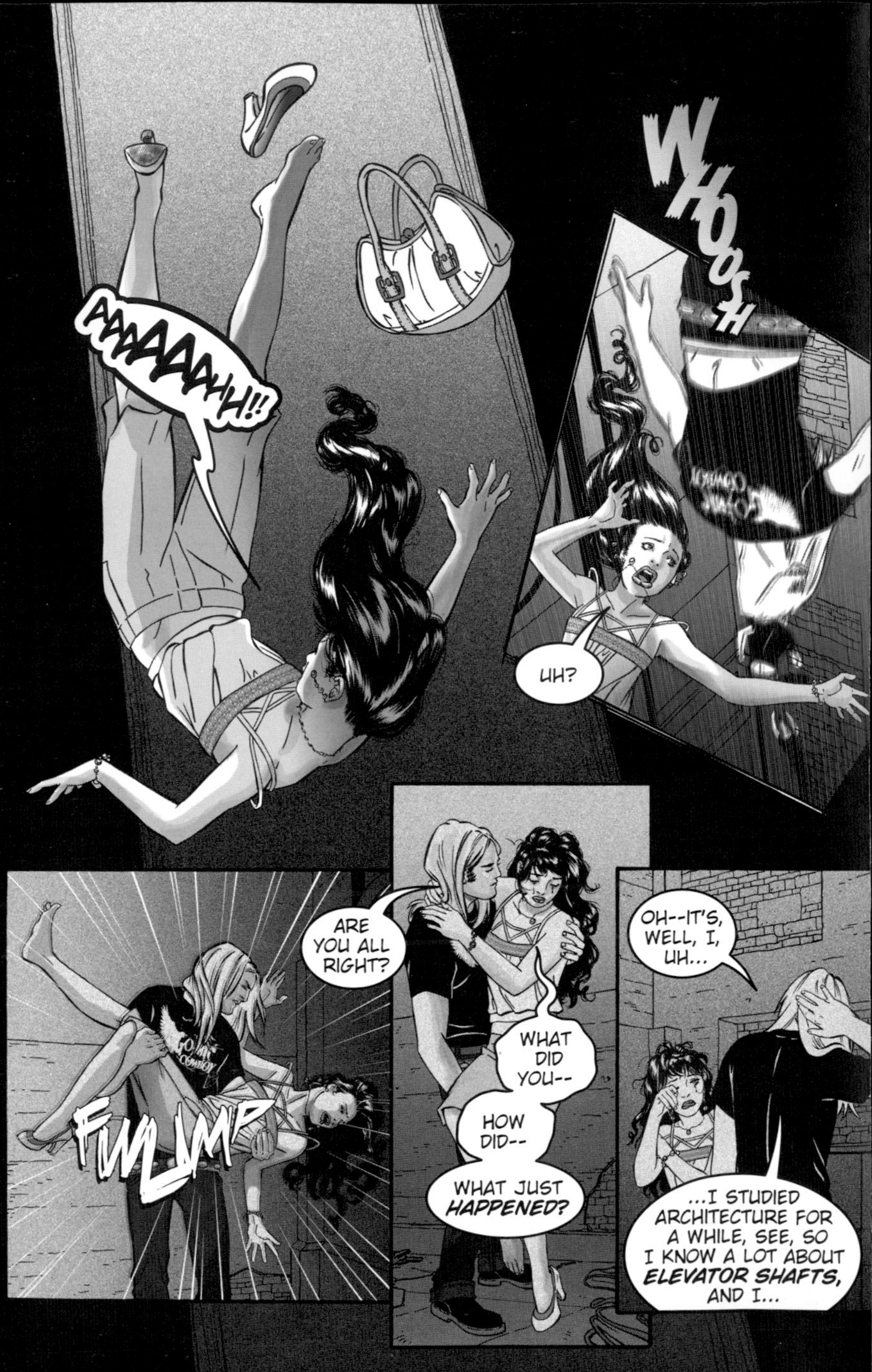
AAAAAAAAHH!!
WHOOSH
UH?
FWUMP
ARE YOU ALL RIGHT?
WHAT DID YOU--
HOW DID--
WHAT JUST *HAPPENED?*
OH--IT'S, WELL, I, UH...
...I STUDIED ARCHITECTURE FOR A WHILE, SEE, SO I KNOW A LOT ABOUT *ELEVATOR SHAFTS,* AND I...

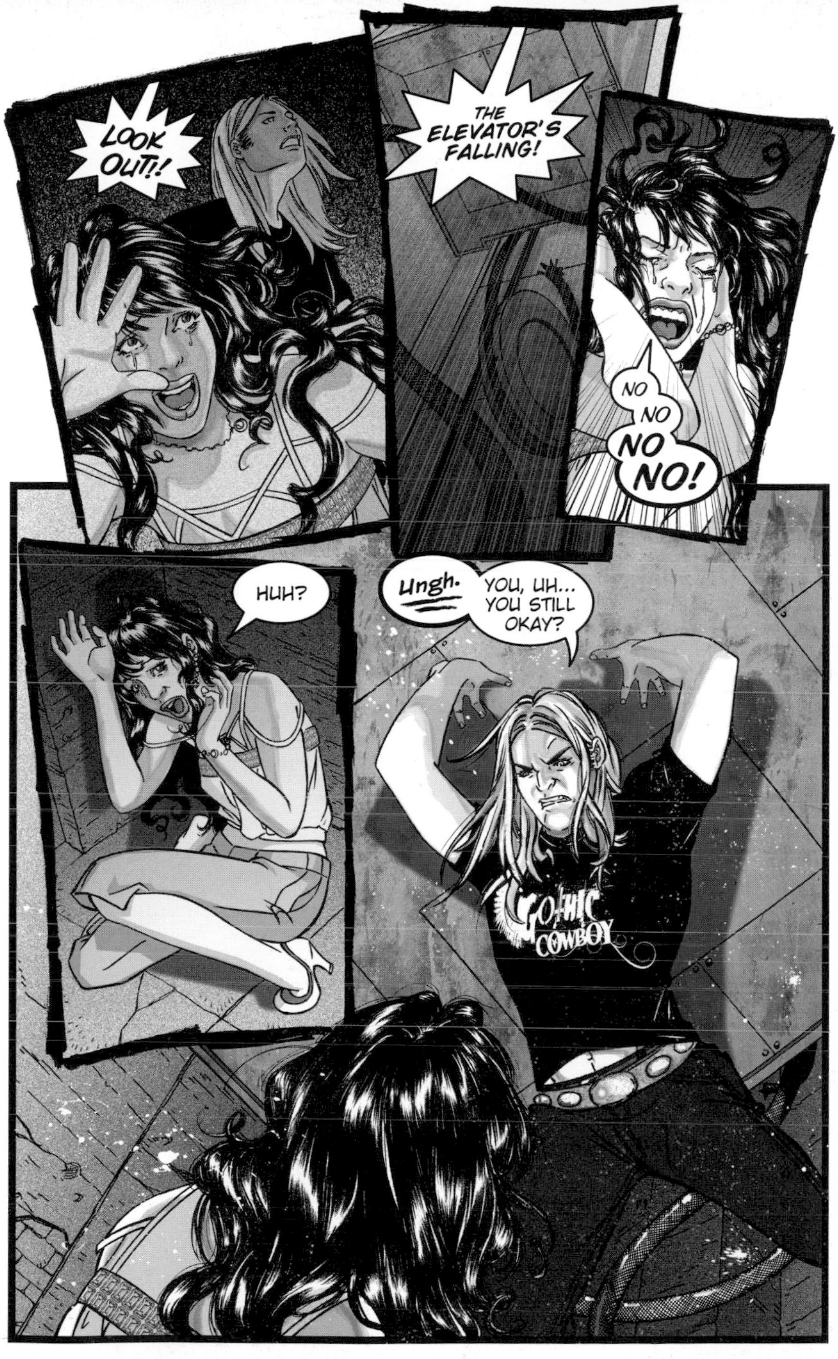
LOOK OUT!!
THE ELEVATOR'S FALLING!
NO NO NO NO!
HUH?
Ungh.
YOU, UH... YOU STILL OKAY?
GOTHIC COWBOY

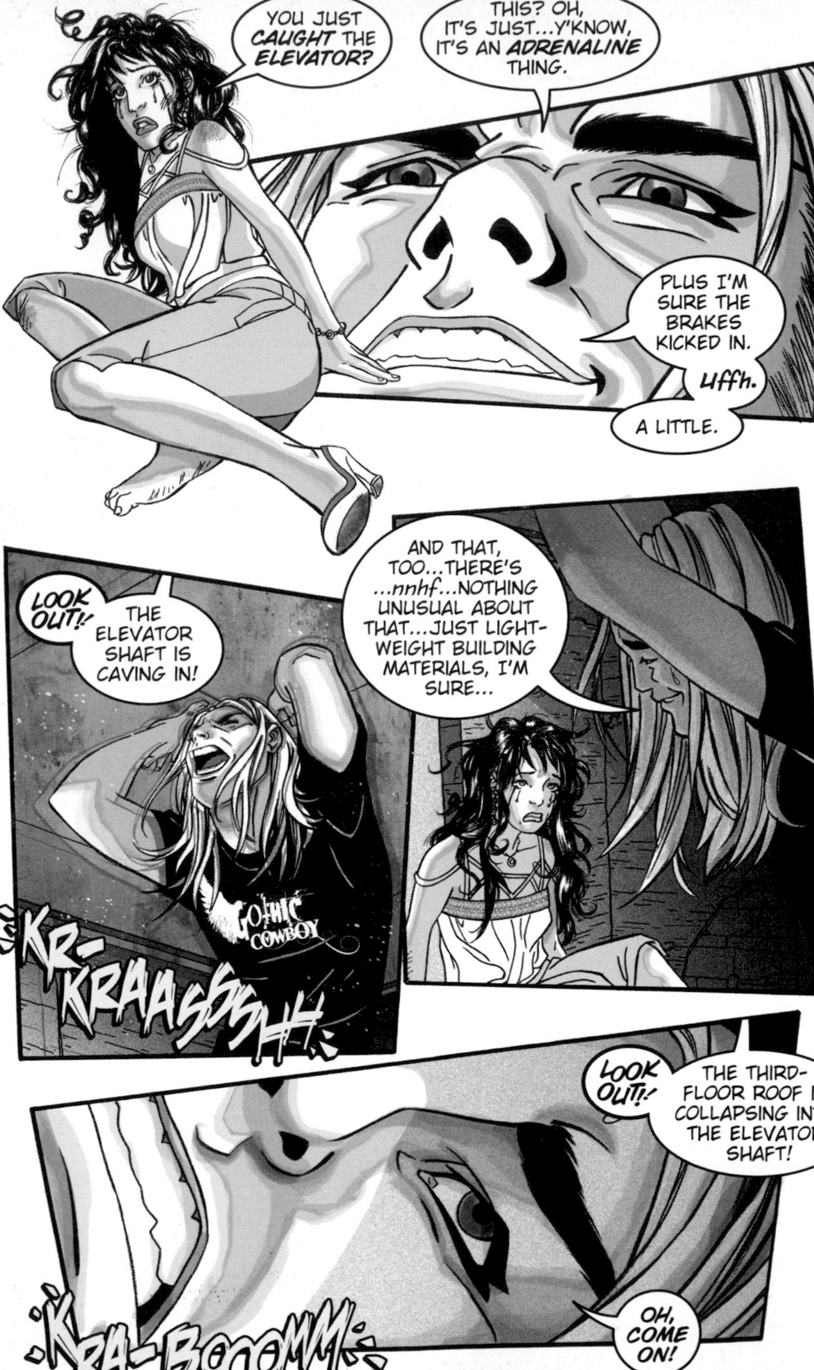
YOU JUST CAUGHT THE ELEVATOR?
THIS? OH, IT'S JUST...Y'KNOW, IT'S AN ADRENALINE THING.
PLUS I'M SURE THE BRAKES KICKED IN.
uffh.
A LITTLE.
LOOK OUT!!
THE ELEVATOR SHAFT IS CAVING IN!
AND THAT, TOO...THERE'S ...nnhf...NOTHING UNUSUAL ABOUT THAT...JUST LIGHT-WEIGHT BUILDING MATERIALS, I'M SURE...
GOTHIC COWBOY
KR-KRAASSSHH!
LOOK OUT!!
THE THIRD-FLOOR ROOF IS COLLAPSING INTO THE ELEVATOR SHAFT!
KRA-BOOOMM!
OH, COME ON!

Chapter 2
Personal Grooming

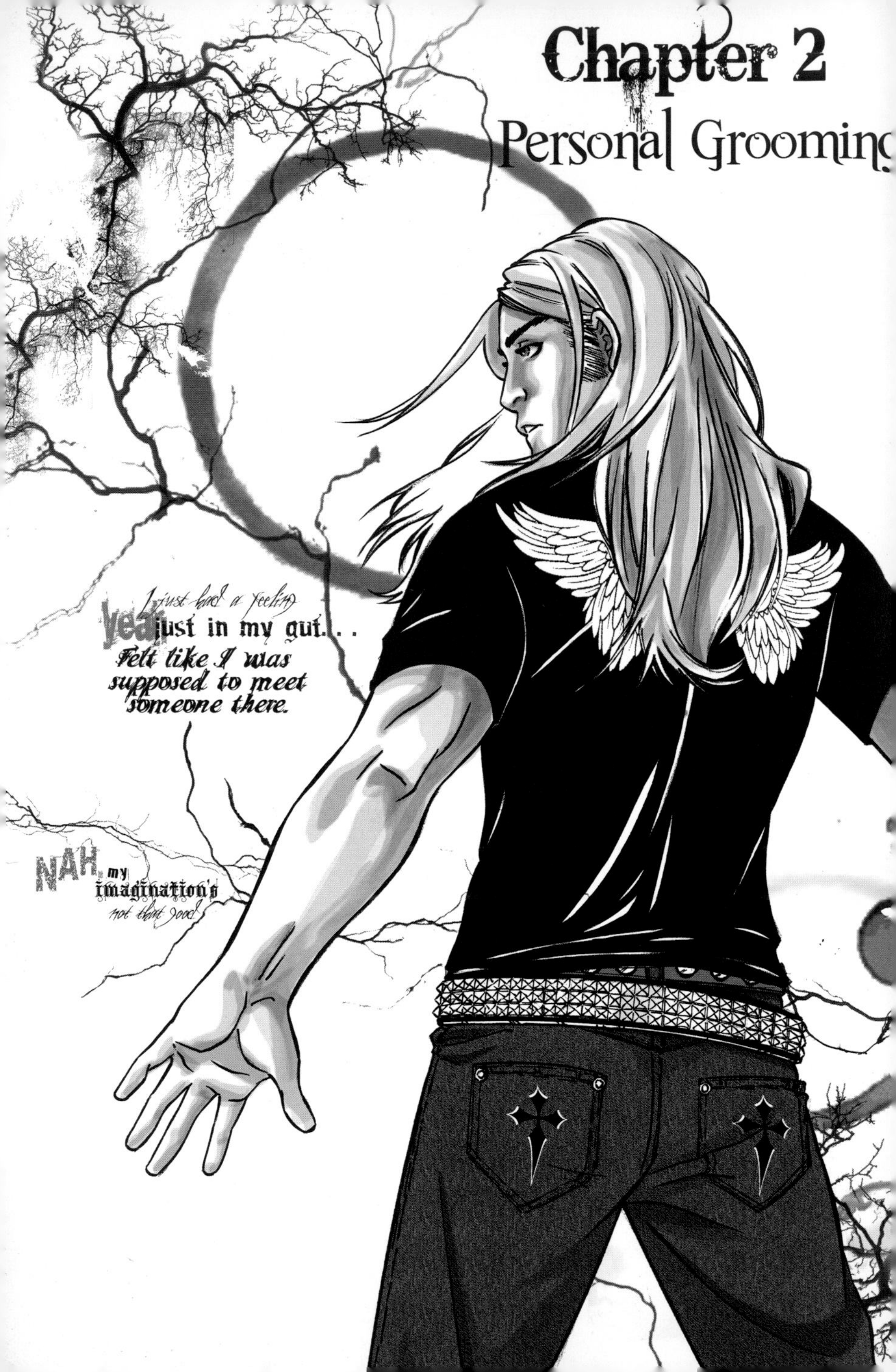
I just had a feeling
yeah just in my gut. . .
Felt like I was supposed to meet someone there.
NAH, my imagination's not that good

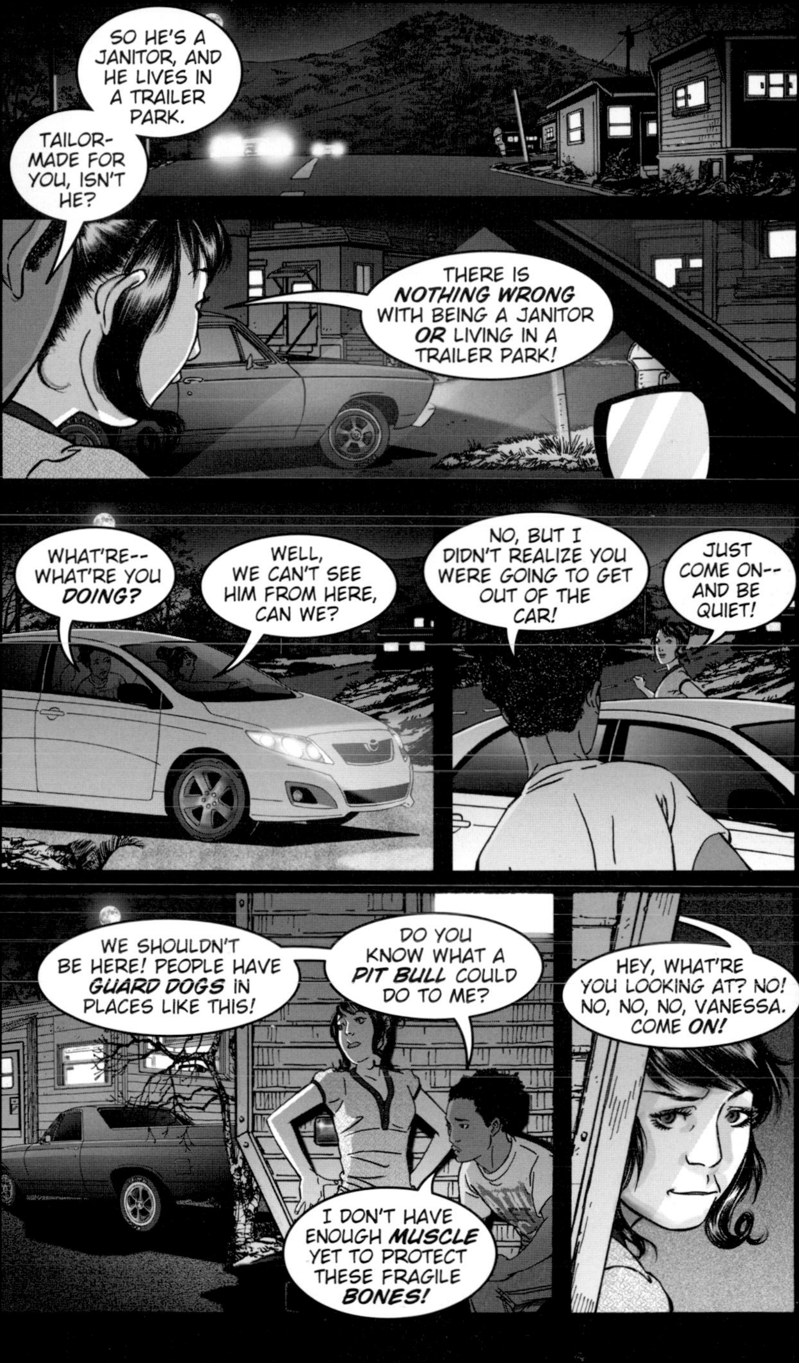
SO HE'S A JANITOR, AND HE LIVES IN A TRAILER PARK.
TAILOR-MADE FOR YOU, ISN'T HE?
THERE IS NOTHING WRONG WITH BEING A JANITOR OR LIVING IN A TRAILER PARK!
WHAT'RE-- WHAT'RE YOU DOING?
WELL, WE CAN'T SEE HIM FROM HERE, CAN WE?
NO, BUT I DIDN'T REALIZE YOU WERE GOING TO GET OUT OF THE CAR!
JUST COME ON-- AND BE QUIET!
WE SHOULDN'T BE HERE! PEOPLE HAVE GUARD DOGS IN PLACES LIKE THIS!
DO YOU KNOW WHAT A PIT BULL COULD DO TO ME?
I DON'T HAVE ENOUGH MUSCLE YET TO PROTECT THESE FRAGILE BONES!
HEY, WHAT'RE YOU LOOKING AT? NO! NO, NO, NO, VANESSA. COME ON!

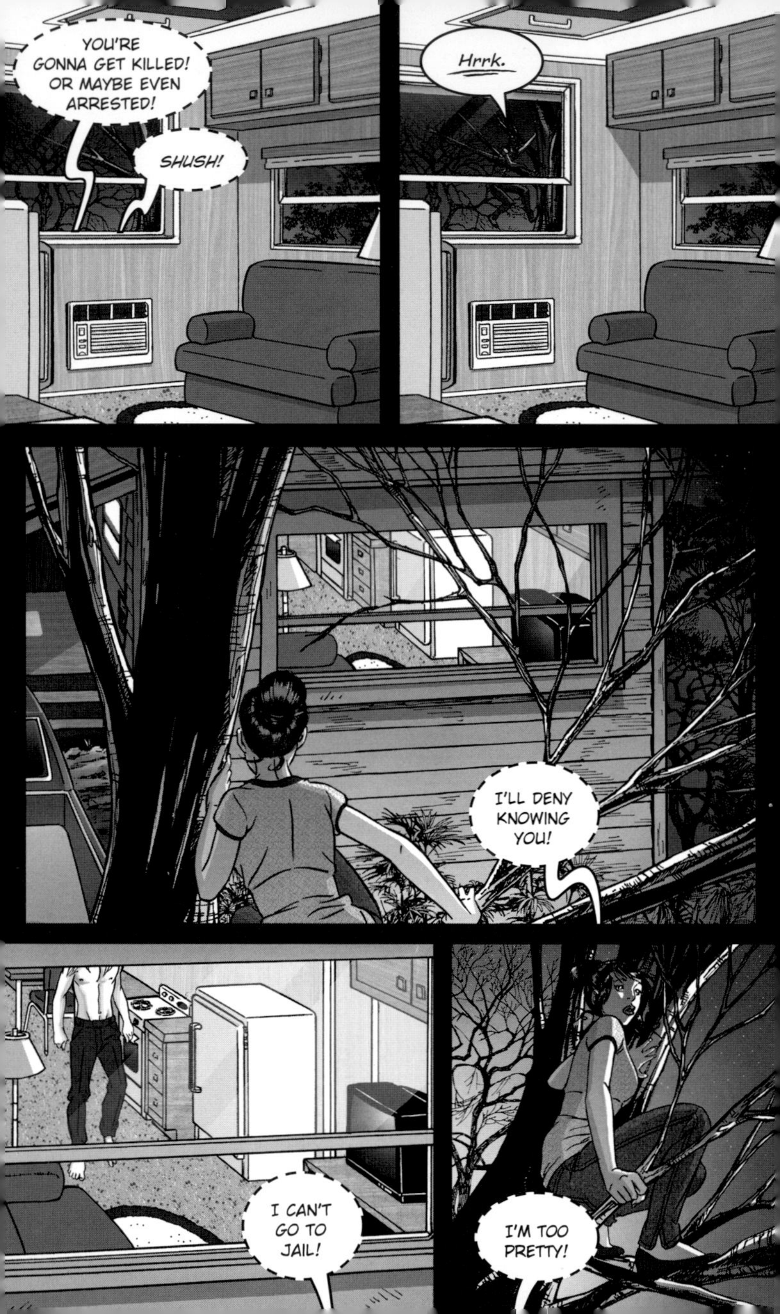

YOU'RE GONNA GET KILLED! OR MAYBE EVEN ARRESTED!
SHUSH!
Hrrk.
I'LL DENY KNOWING YOU!
I CAN'T GO TO JAIL!
I'M TOO PRETTY!

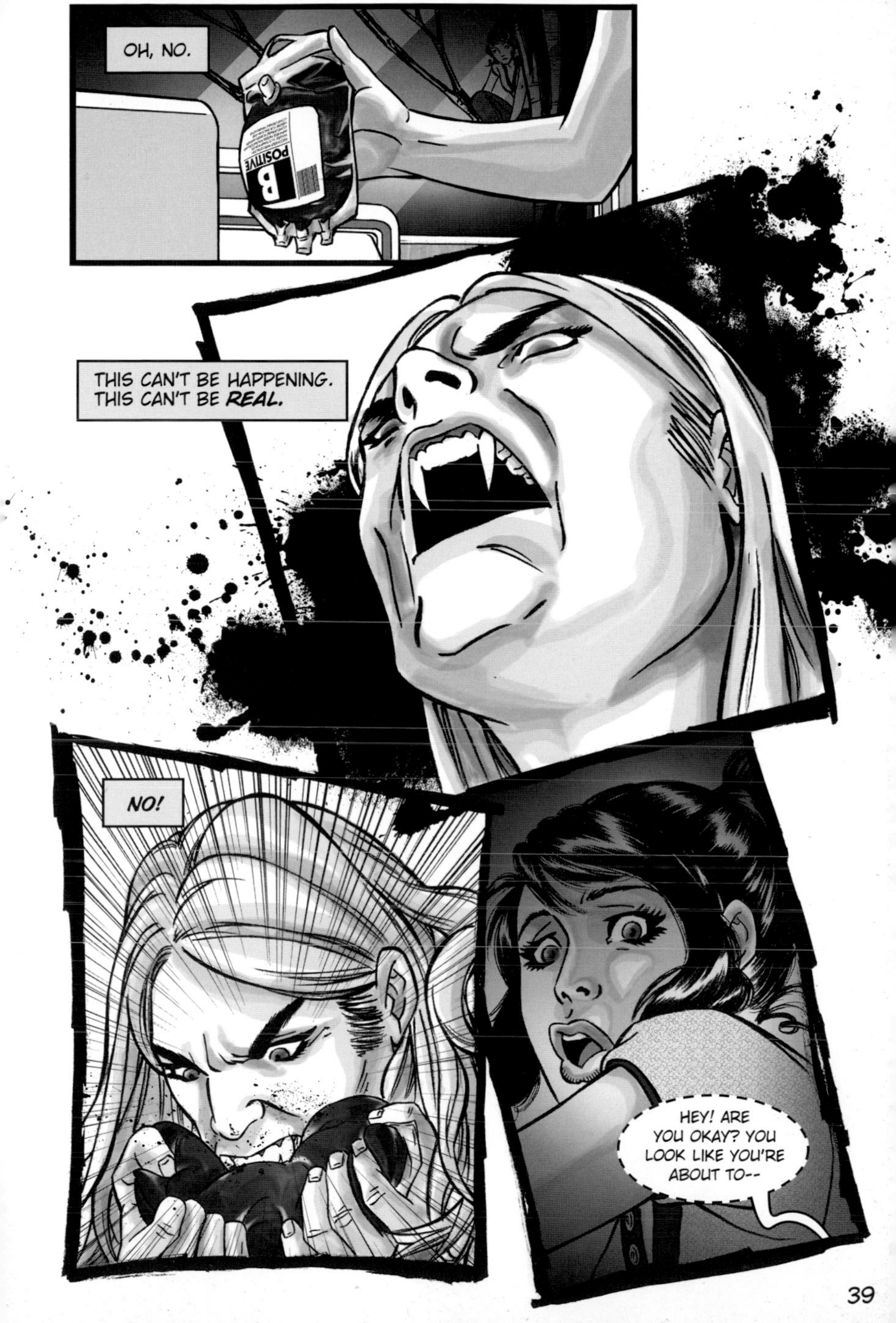
OH, NO.
B POSITIVE
THIS CAN'T BE HAPPENING. THIS CAN'T BE *REAL.*
NO!
HEY! ARE YOU OKAY? YOU LOOK LIKE YOU'RE ABOUT TO--

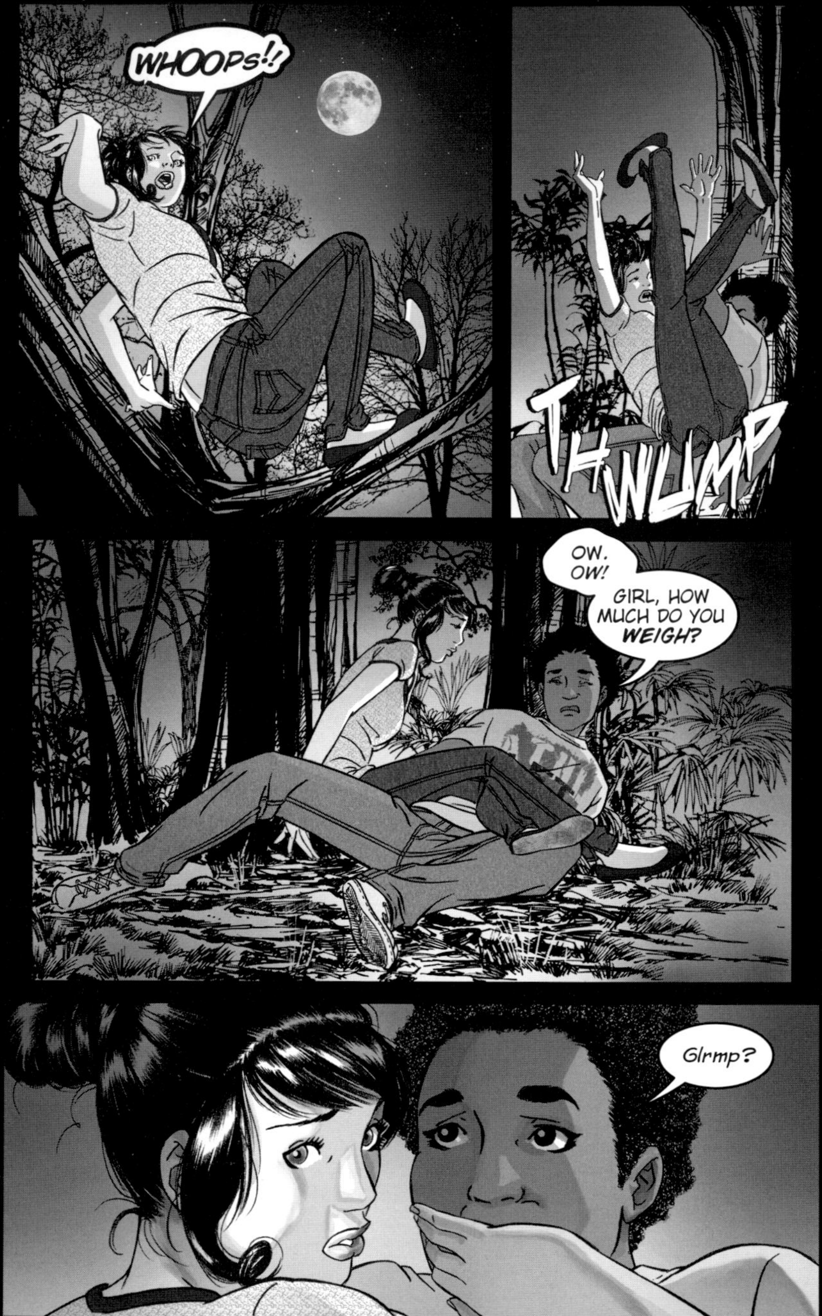
WHOOPS!!
THWUMP
OW. OW!
GIRL, HOW MUCH DO YOU WEIGH?
Glrmp?

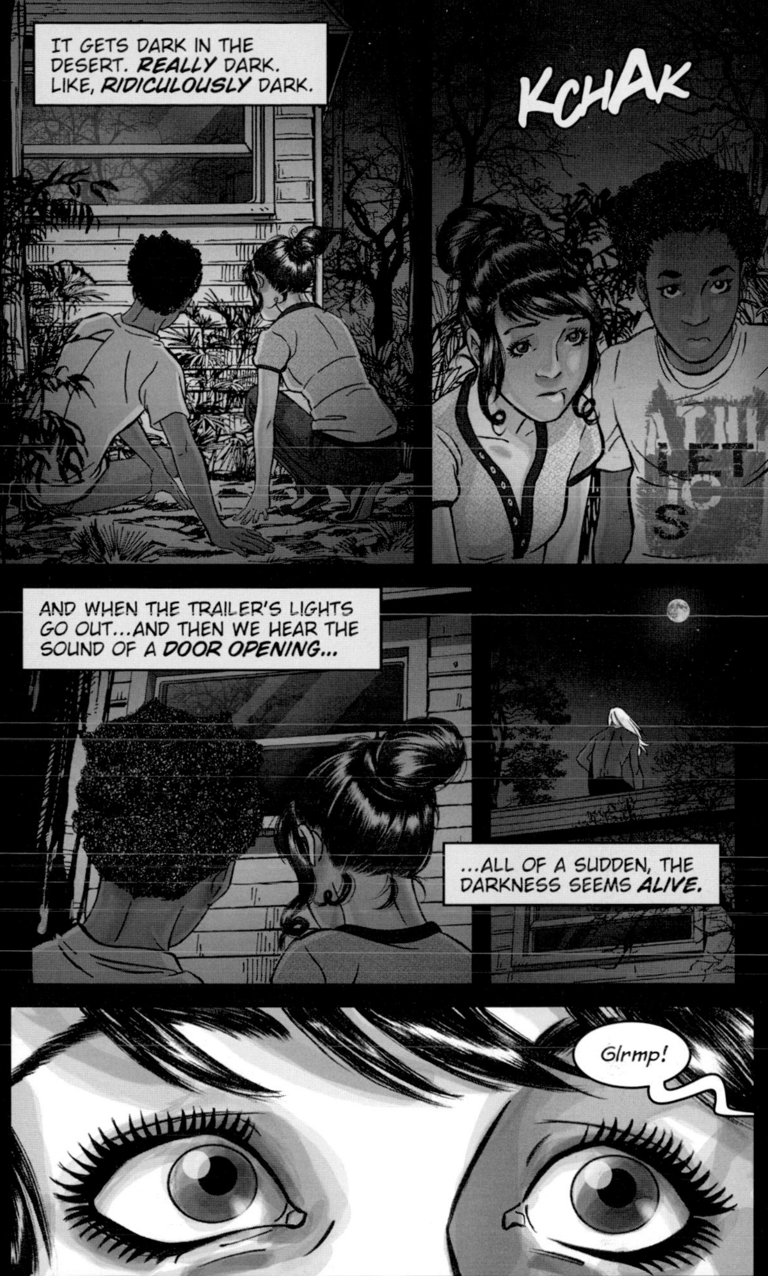
IT GETS DARK IN THE DESERT. REALLY DARK. LIKE, RIDICULOUSLY DARK.
KCHAK
AND WHEN THE TRAILER'S LIGHTS GO OUT...AND THEN WE HEAR THE SOUND OF A DOOR OPENING...
...ALL OF A SUDDEN, THE DARKNESS SEEMS ALIVE.
Glrmp!

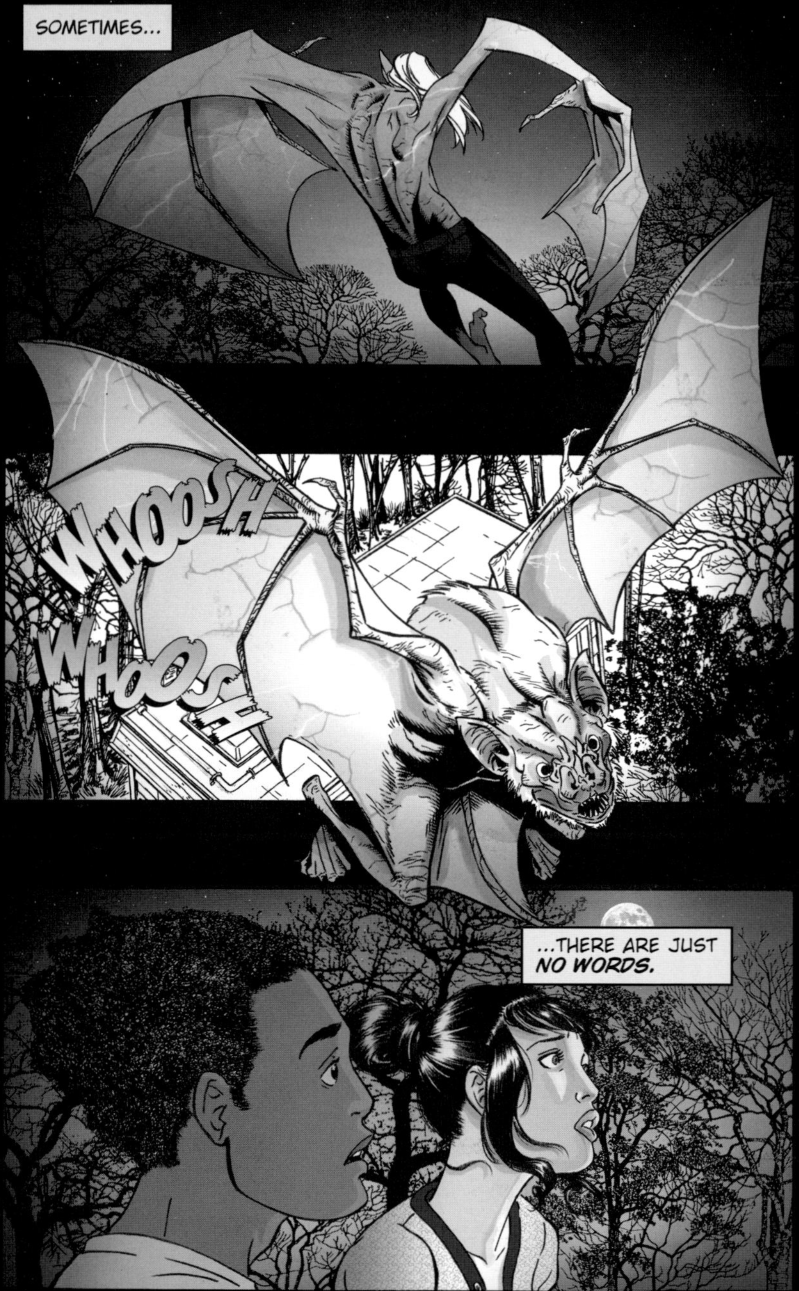
SOMETIMES...
WHOOSH
WHOOSH
...THERE ARE JUST NO WORDS.

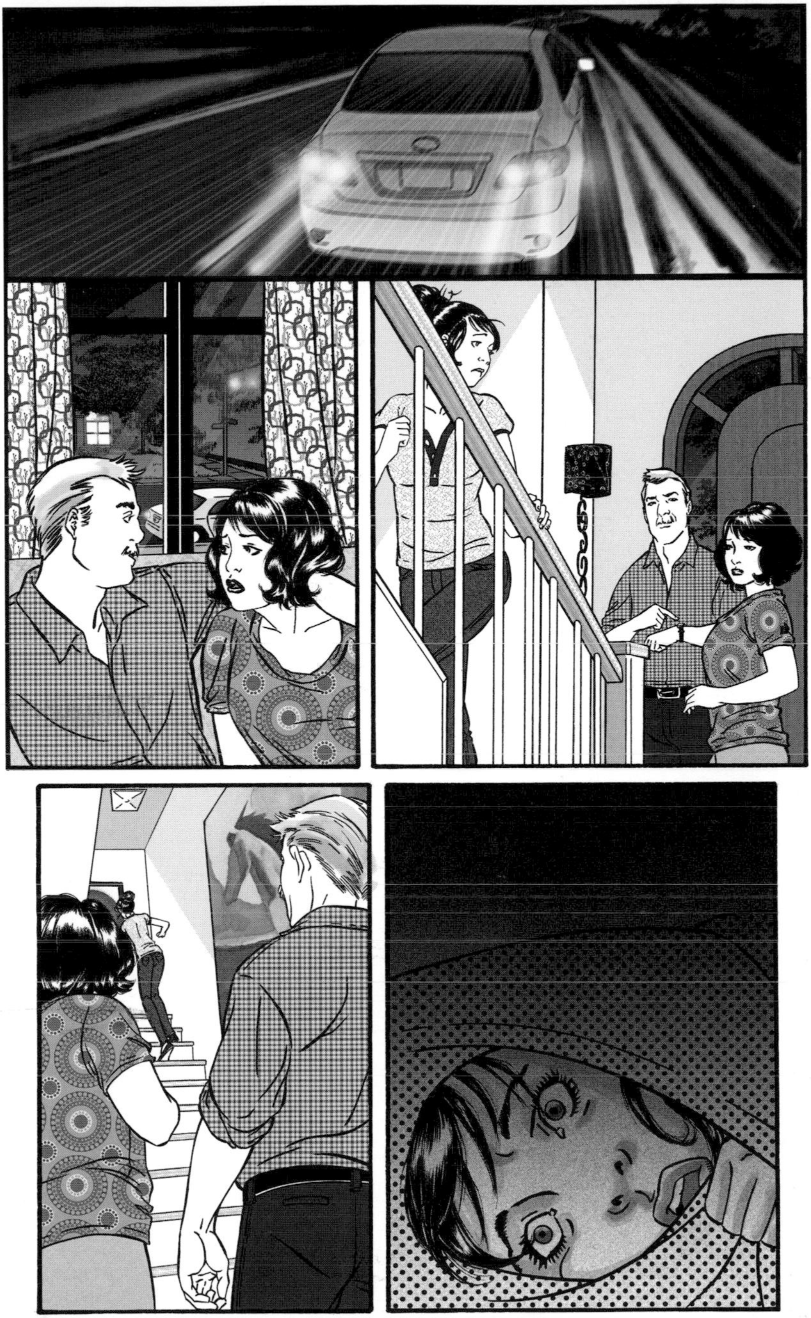

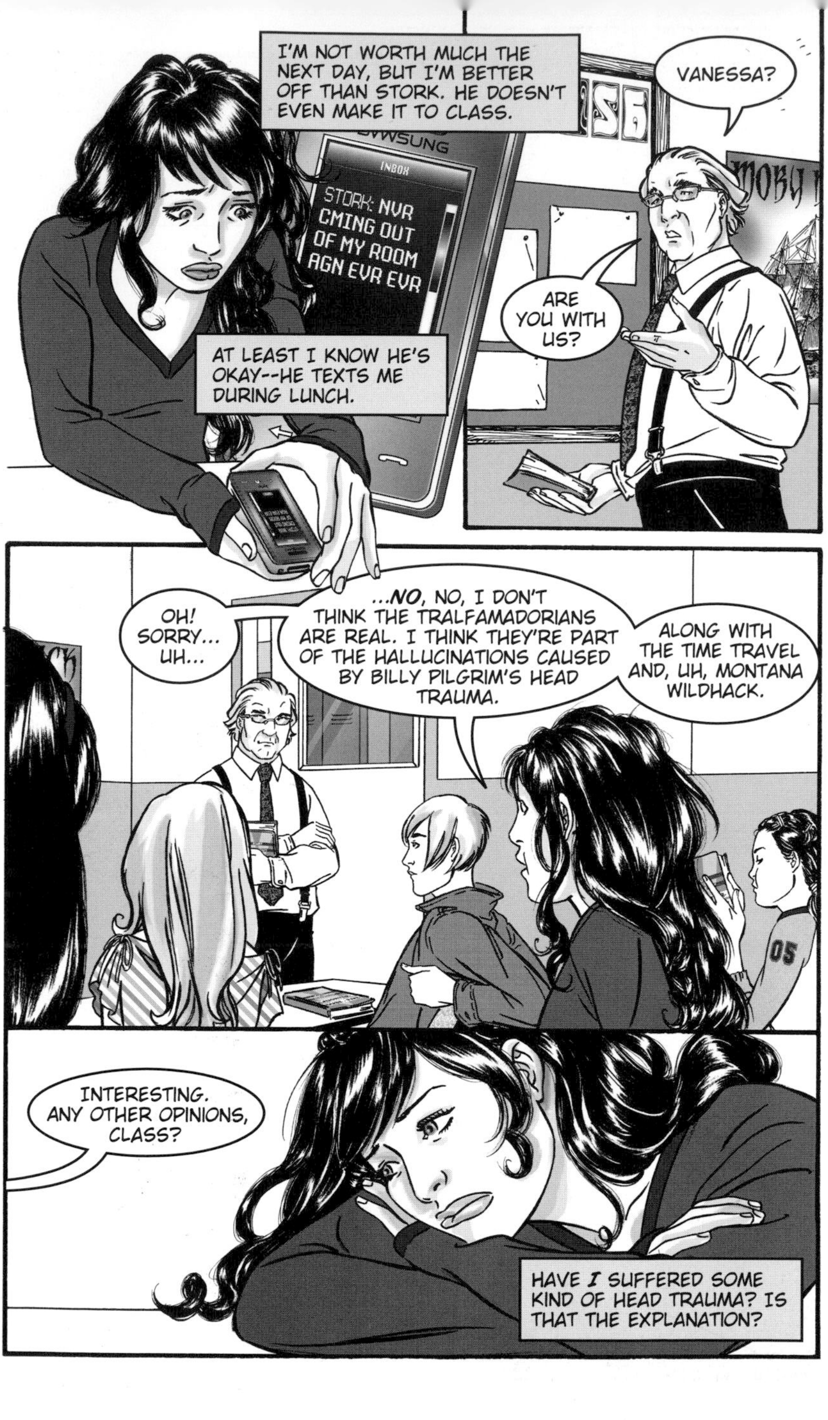
I'M NOT WORTH MUCH THE NEXT DAY, BUT I'M BETTER OFF THAN STORK. HE DOESN'T EVEN MAKE IT TO CLASS.
INBOX
STORK: NVR CMING OUT OF MY ROOM AGN EVR EVR
AT LEAST I KNOW HE'S OKAY--HE TEXTS ME DURING LUNCH.
VANESSA?
ARE YOU WITH US?
OH! SORRY... UH...
...**NO**, NO, I DON'T THINK THE TRALFAMADORIANS ARE REAL. I THINK THEY'RE PART OF THE HALLUCINATIONS CAUSED BY BILLY PILGRIM'S HEAD TRAUMA.
ALONG WITH THE TIME TRAVEL AND, UH, MONTANA WILDHACK.
INTERESTING. ANY OTHER OPINIONS, CLASS?
HAVE *I* SUFFERED SOME KIND OF HEAD TRAUMA? IS THAT THE EXPLANATION?

45

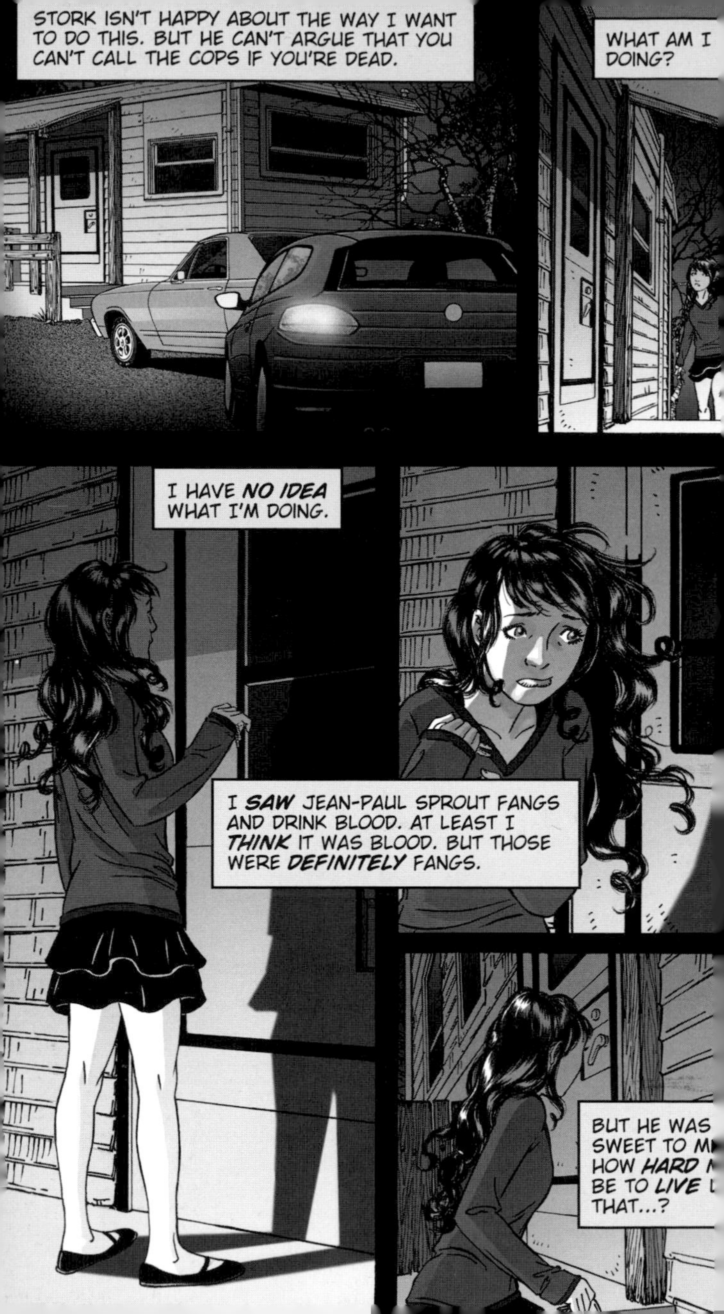
STORK ISN'T HAPPY ABOUT THE WAY I WANT TO DO THIS. BUT HE CAN'T ARGUE THAT YOU CAN'T CALL THE COPS IF YOU'RE DEAD.
WHAT AM I DOING?
I HAVE NO IDEA WHAT I'M DOING.
I SAW JEAN-PAUL SPROUT FANGS AND DRINK BLOOD. AT LEAST I THINK IT WAS BLOOD. BUT THOSE WERE DEFINITELY FANGS.
BUT HE WAS SWEET TO M HOW HARD BE TO LIVE THAT...?

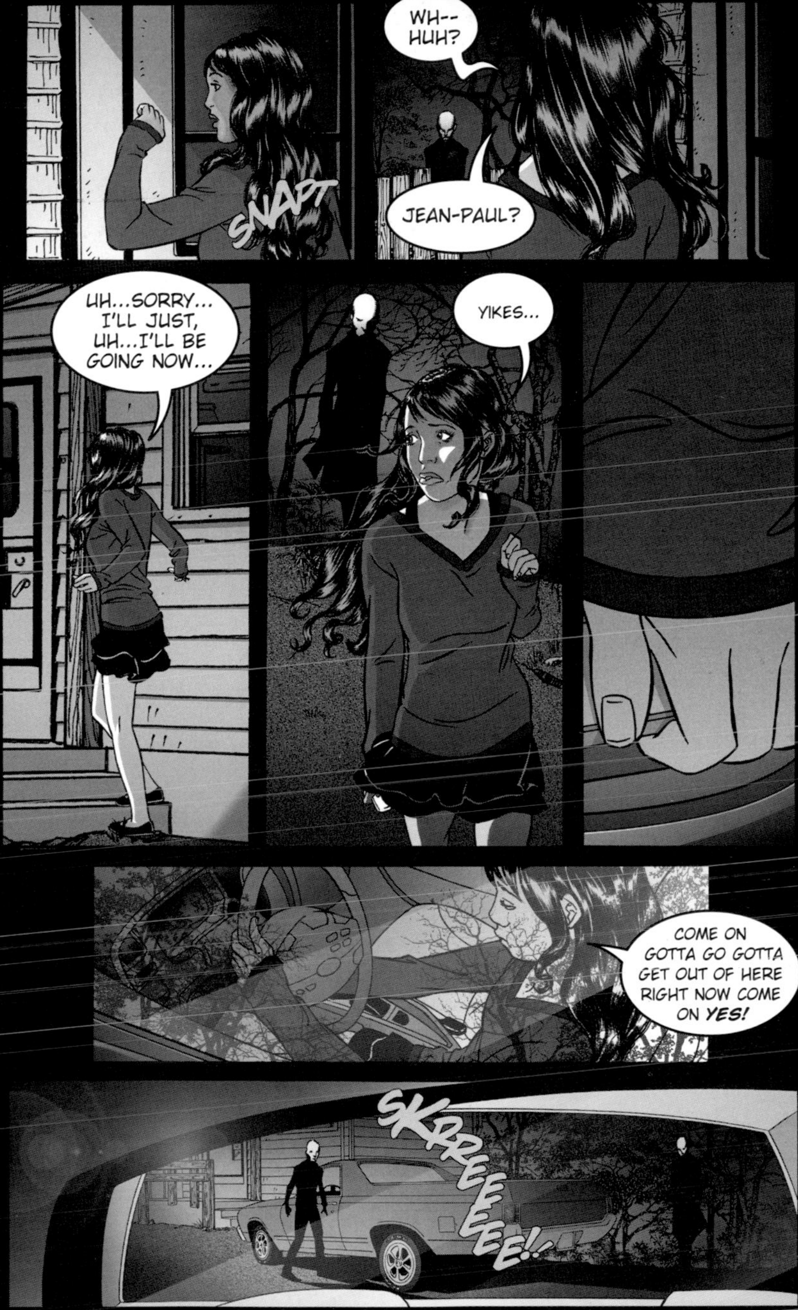
SNAPT
WH--
HUH?
JEAN-PAUL?
UH...SORRY...
I'LL JUST,
UH...I'LL BE
GOING NOW...
YIKES...
COME ON
GOTTA GO GOTTA
GET OUT OF HERE
RIGHT NOW COME
ON *YES!*
SKREEEEEE!!

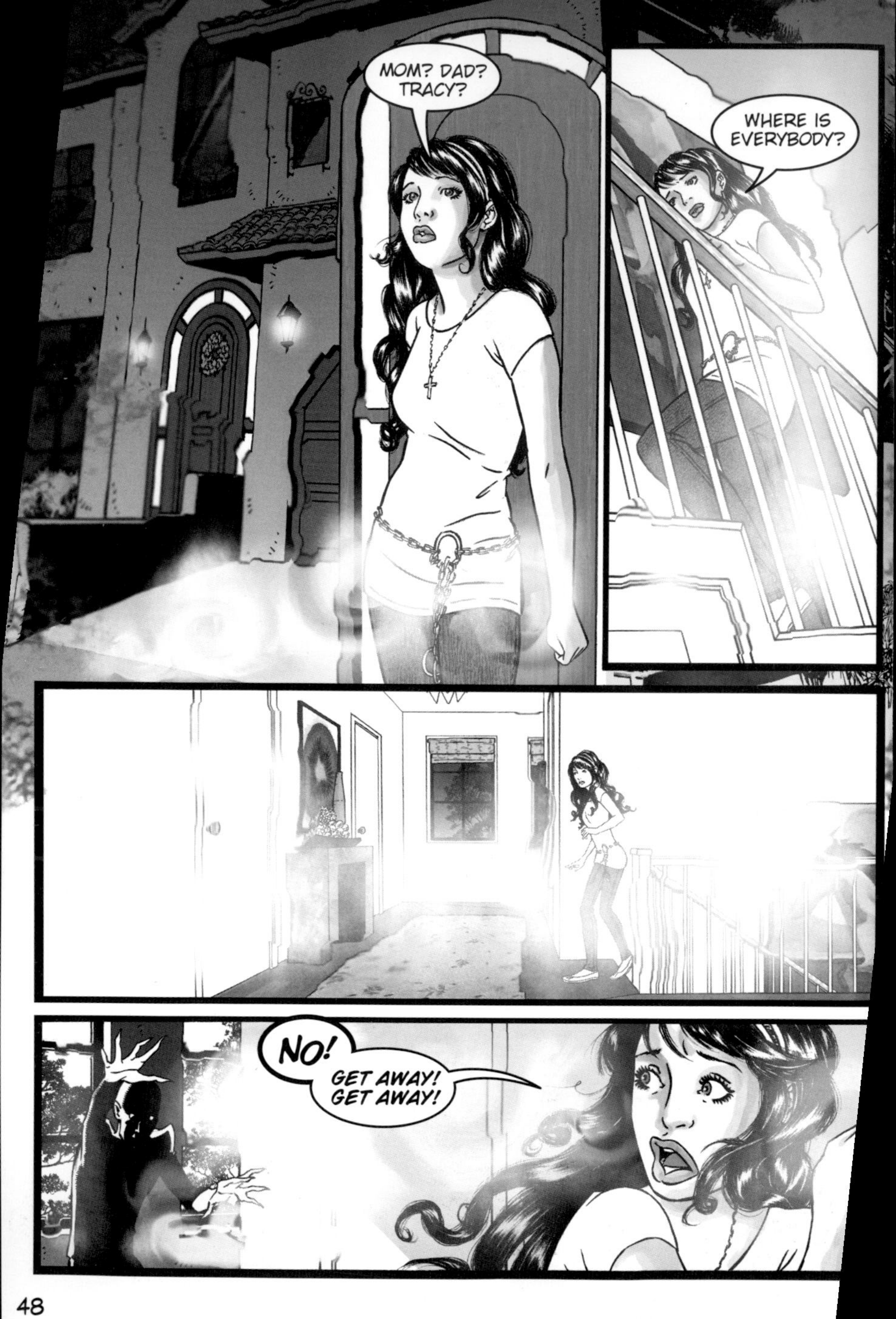
MOM? DAD? TRACY?
WHERE IS EVERYBODY?
NO!
GET AWAY! GET AWAY!

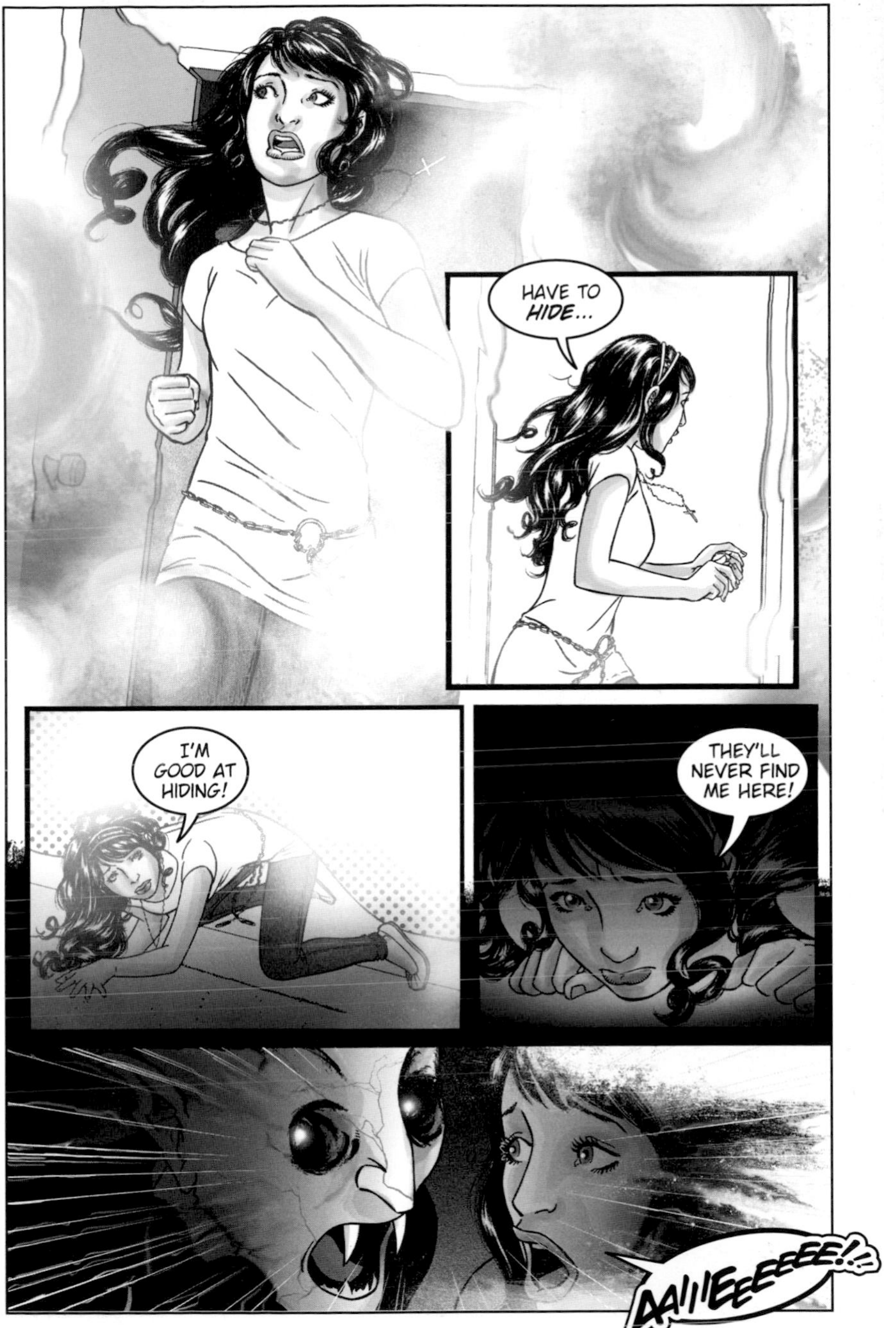
HAVE TO HIDE...
I'M GOOD AT HIDING!
THEY'LL NEVER FIND ME HERE!
AAIIIEEEEEEE!!

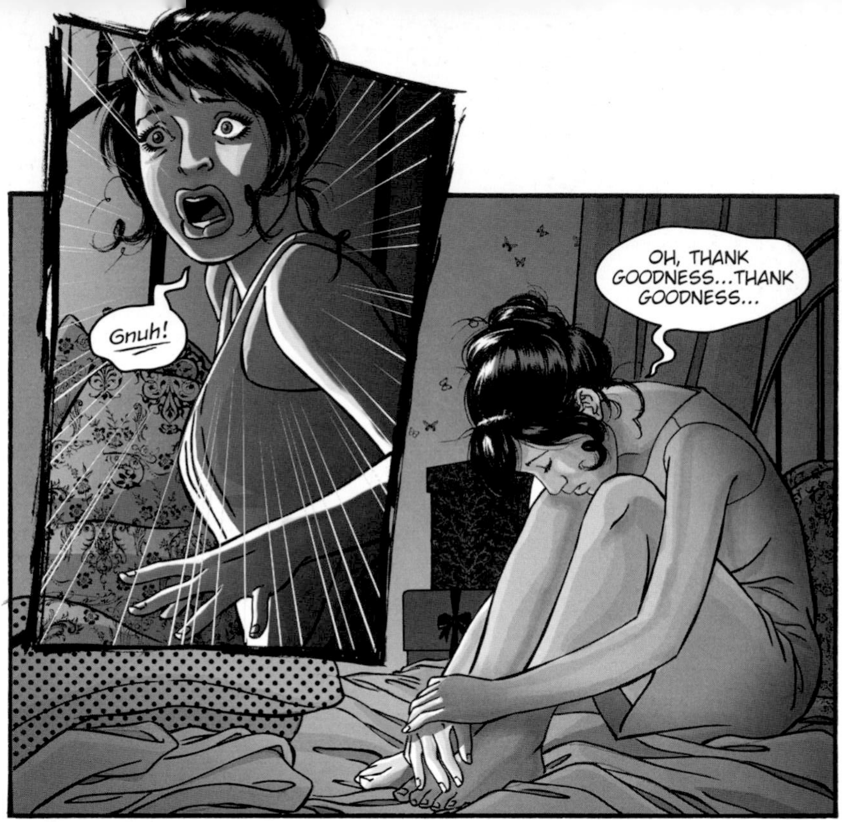
Gnuh!
OH, THANK GOODNESS...THANK GOODNESS...

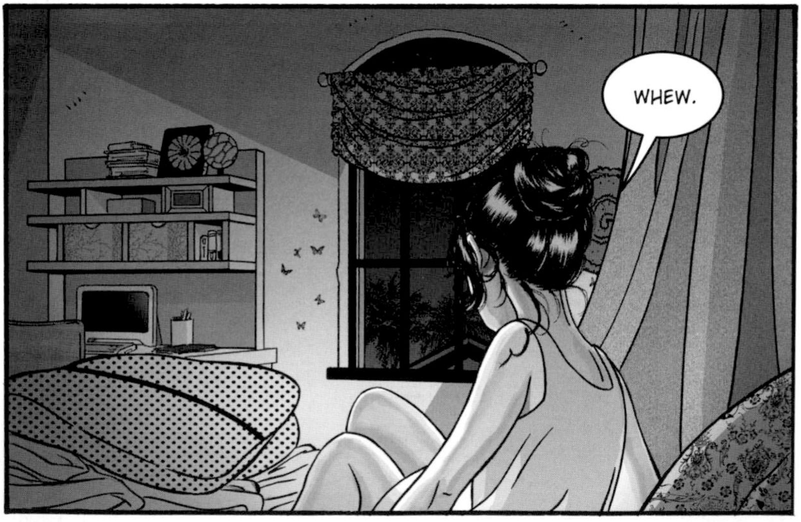
WHEW.

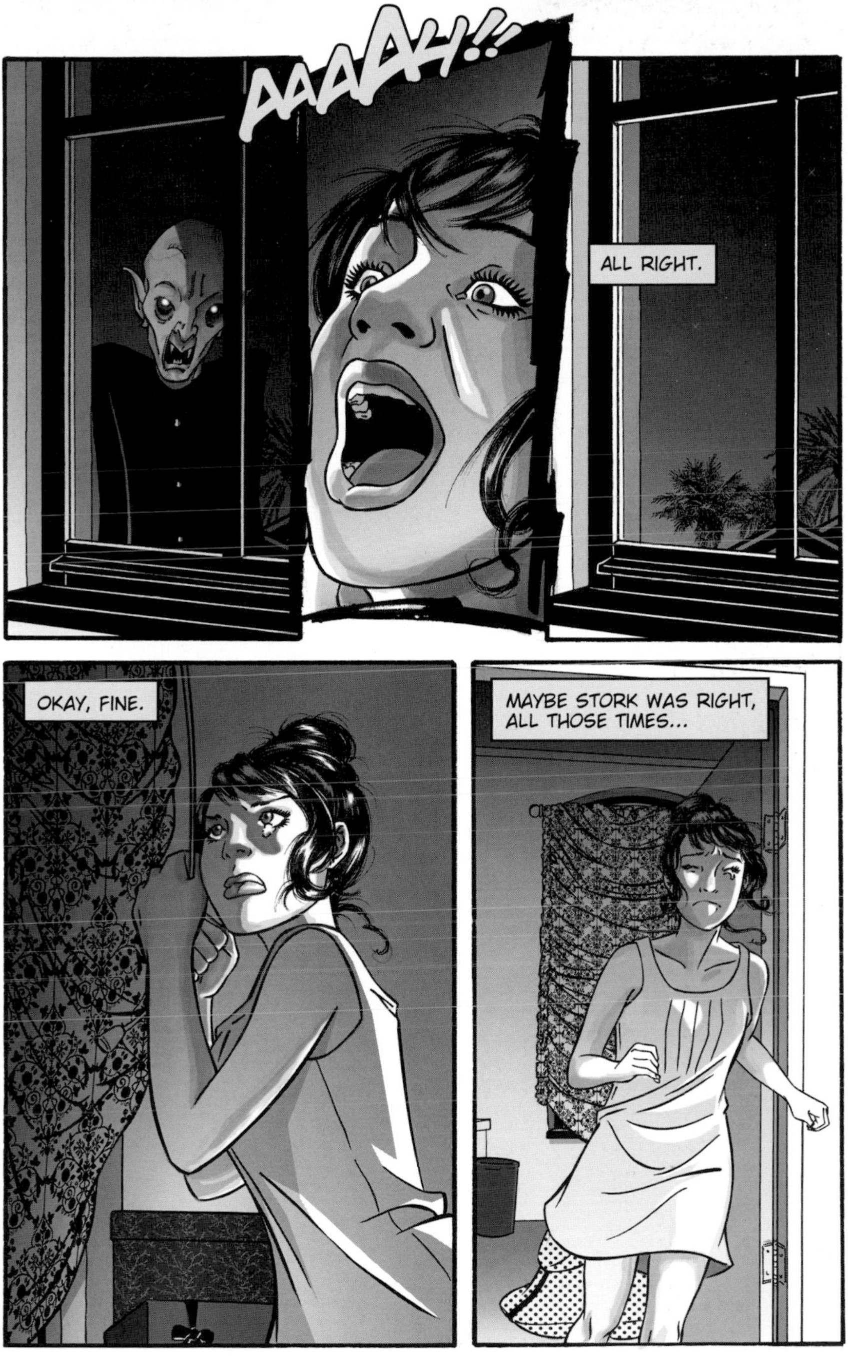
AAAAH!!
ALL RIGHT.
OKAY, FINE.
MAYBE STORK WAS RIGHT, ALL THOSE TIMES...

...HE TOLD ME I NEEDED *PROFESSIONAL HELP.*

OF COURSE, GIVEN MY LIMITED RESOURCES AND TIME CONSTRAINTS...

GO SQUID!

...THE BEST I CAN DO IS *MR. BARRY,* MY GUIDANCE COUNSELOR.

WISH STORK COULD BE HERE WITH ME...HIS MOM CAN REALLY PICK GREAT TIMES TO SEND HIM RUNNING ERRANDS.

VANESSA?

COME ON IN, PLEASE!

MAKE YOURSELF COMFORTABLE.

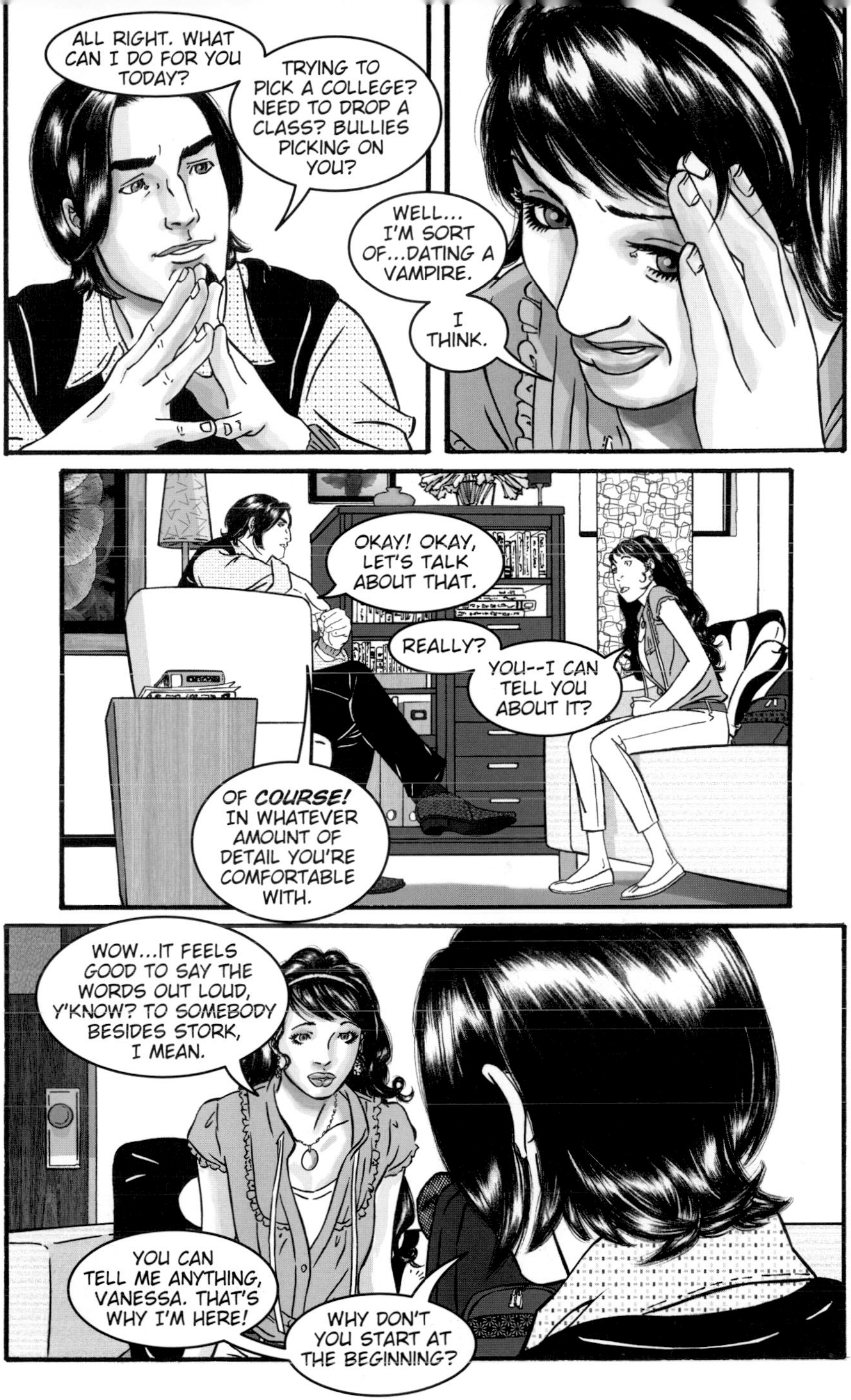
ALL RIGHT. WHAT CAN I DO FOR YOU TODAY?
TRYING TO PICK A COLLEGE? NEED TO DROP A CLASS? BULLIES PICKING ON YOU?
WELL... I'M SORT OF...DATING A VAMPIRE.
I THINK.
OKAY! OKAY, LET'S TALK ABOUT THAT.
REALLY?
YOU--I CAN TELL YOU ABOUT IT?
OF COURSE! IN WHATEVER AMOUNT OF DETAIL YOU'RE COMFORTABLE WITH.
WOW...IT FEELS GOOD TO SAY THE WORDS OUT LOUD, Y'KNOW? TO SOMEBODY BESIDES STORK, I MEAN.
YOU CAN TELL ME ANYTHING, VANESSA. THAT'S WHY I'M HERE!
WHY DON'T YOU START AT THE BEGINNING?

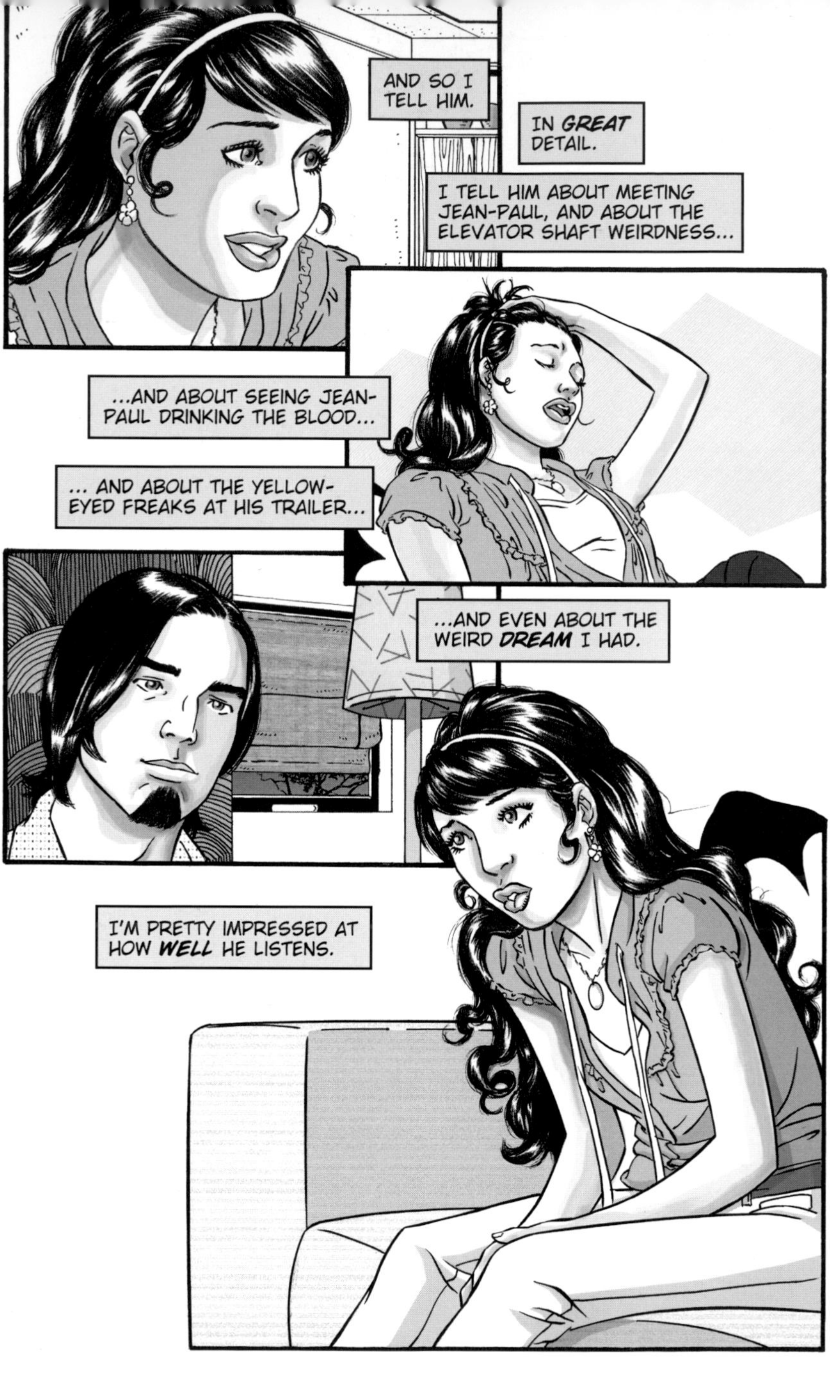
AND SO I TELL HIM.
IN GREAT DETAIL.
I TELL HIM ABOUT MEETING JEAN-PAUL, AND ABOUT THE ELEVATOR SHAFT WEIRDNESS...
...AND ABOUT SEEING JEAN-PAUL DRINKING THE BLOOD...
... AND ABOUT THE YELLOW-EYED FREAKS AT HIS TRAILER...
...AND EVEN ABOUT THE WEIRD DREAM I HAD.
I'M PRETTY IMPRESSED AT HOW WELL HE LISTENS.

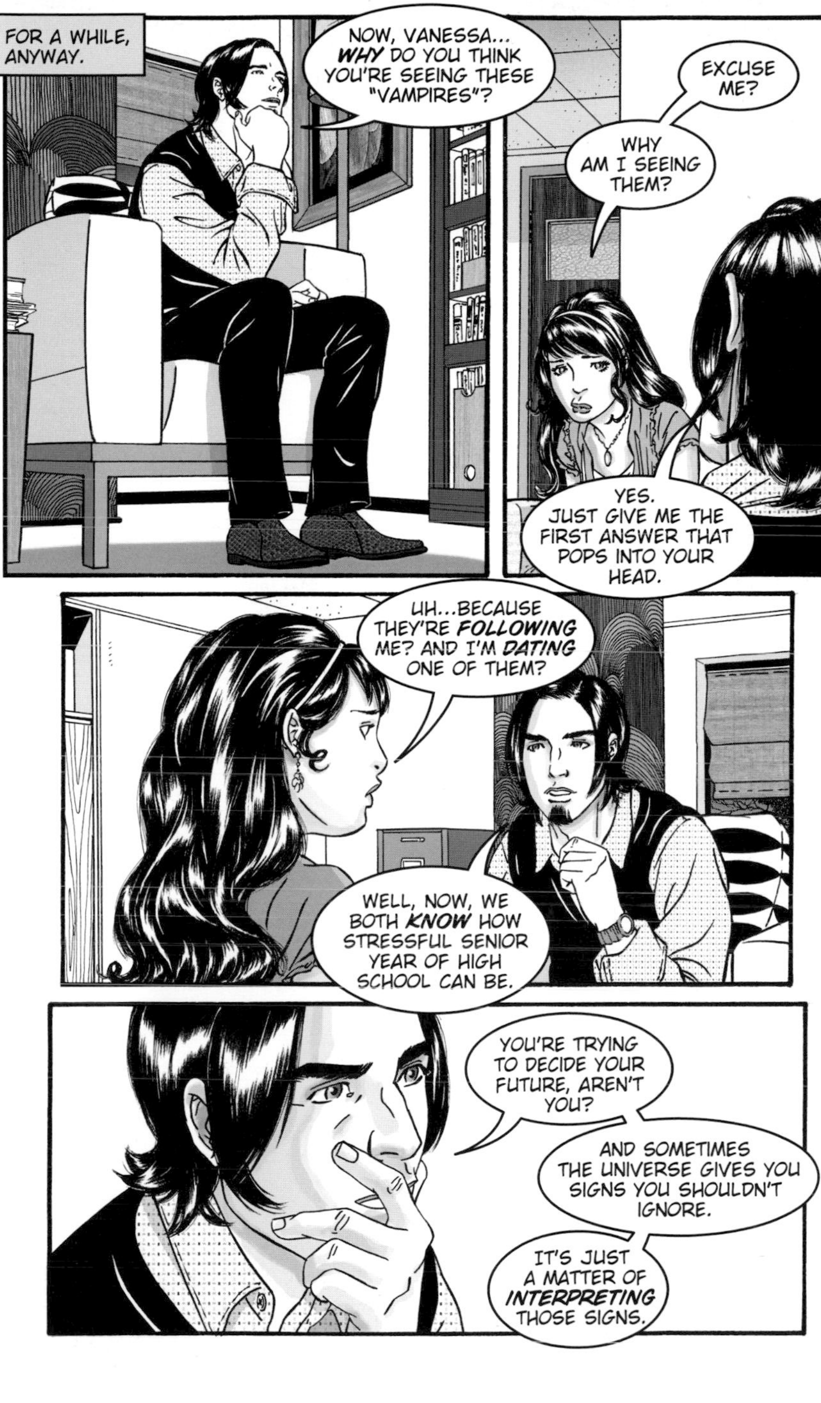

FOR A WHILE, ANYWAY.
NOW, VANESSA... *WHY* DO YOU THINK YOU'RE SEEING THESE "VAMPIRES"?
EXCUSE ME?
WHY AM I SEEING THEM?
YES. JUST GIVE ME THE FIRST ANSWER THAT POPS INTO YOUR HEAD.
UH...BECAUSE THEY'RE *FOLLOWING* ME? AND I'M *DATING* ONE OF THEM?
WELL, NOW, WE BOTH *KNOW* HOW STRESSFUL SENIOR YEAR OF HIGH SCHOOL CAN BE.
YOU'RE TRYING TO DECIDE YOUR FUTURE, AREN'T YOU?
AND SOMETIMES THE UNIVERSE GIVES YOU SIGNS YOU SHOULDN'T IGNORE.
IT'S JUST A MATTER OF *INTERPRETING* THOSE SIGNS.

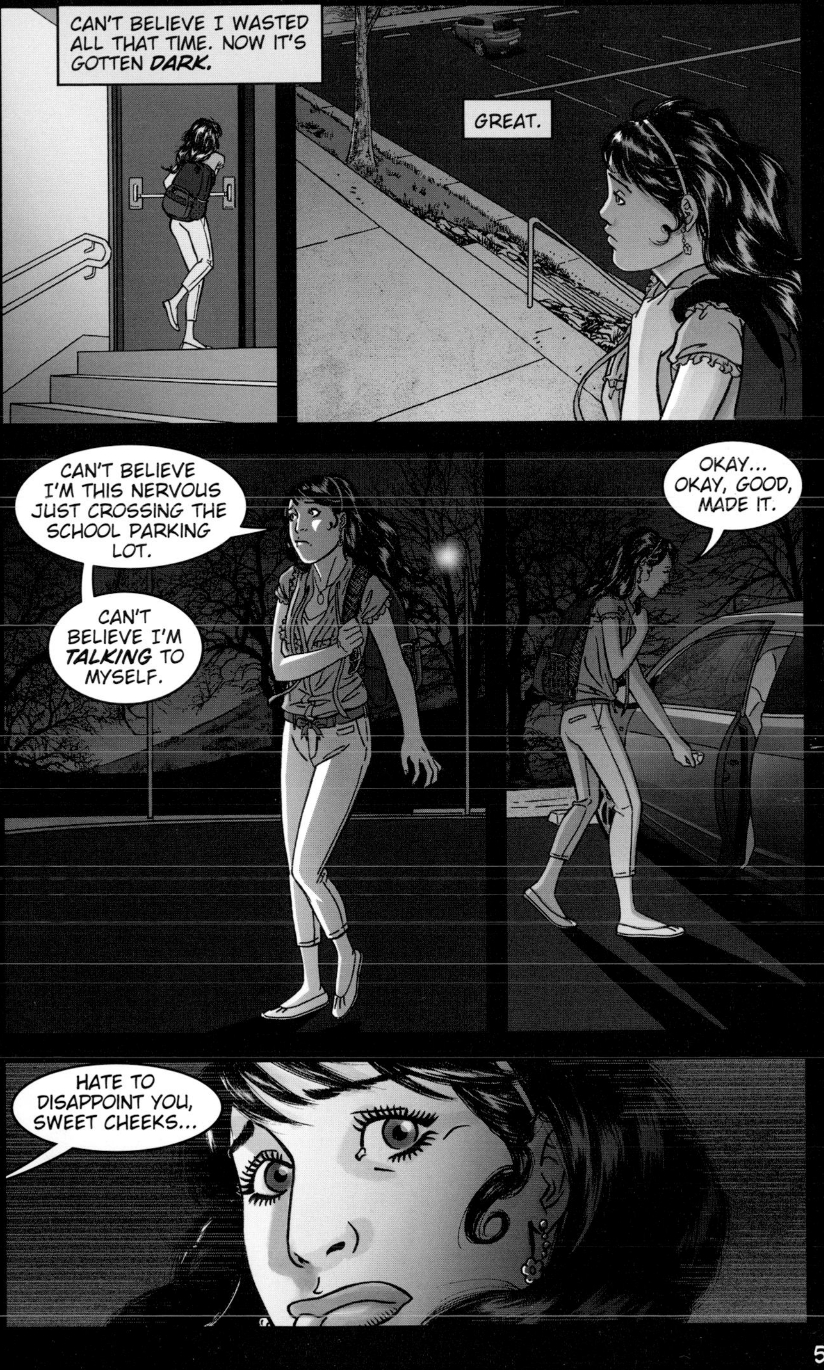
CAN'T BELIEVE I WASTED ALL THAT TIME. NOW IT'S GOTTEN DARK.
GREAT.
CAN'T BELIEVE I'M THIS NERVOUS JUST CROSSING THE SCHOOL PARKING LOT.
CAN'T BELIEVE I'M TALKING TO MYSELF.
OKAY... OKAY, GOOD, MADE IT.
HATE TO DISAPPOINT YOU, SWEET CHEEKS...

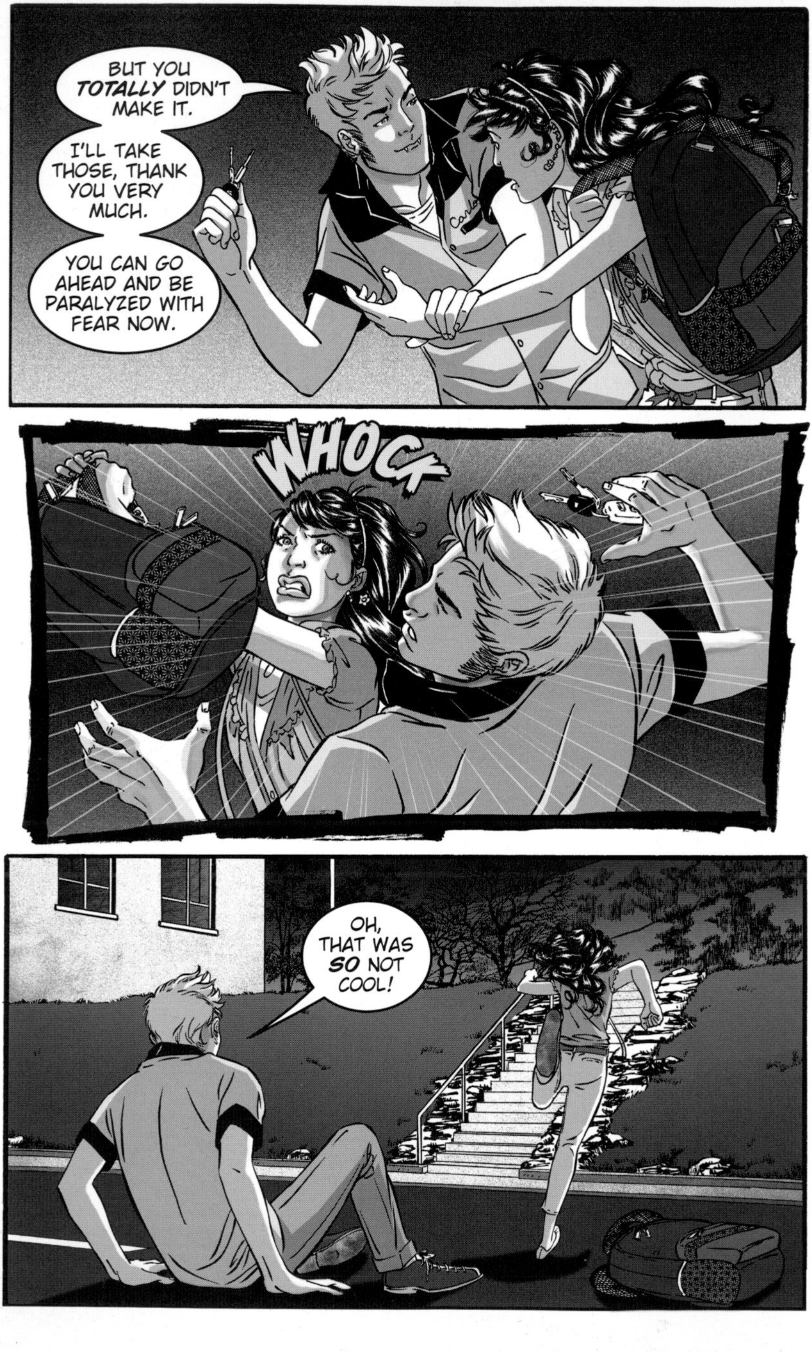

BUT YOU TOTALLY DIDN'T MAKE IT.
I'LL TAKE THOSE, THANK YOU VERY MUCH.
YOU CAN GO AHEAD AND BE PARALYZED WITH FEAR NOW.
WHOCK
OH, THAT WAS SO NOT COOL!

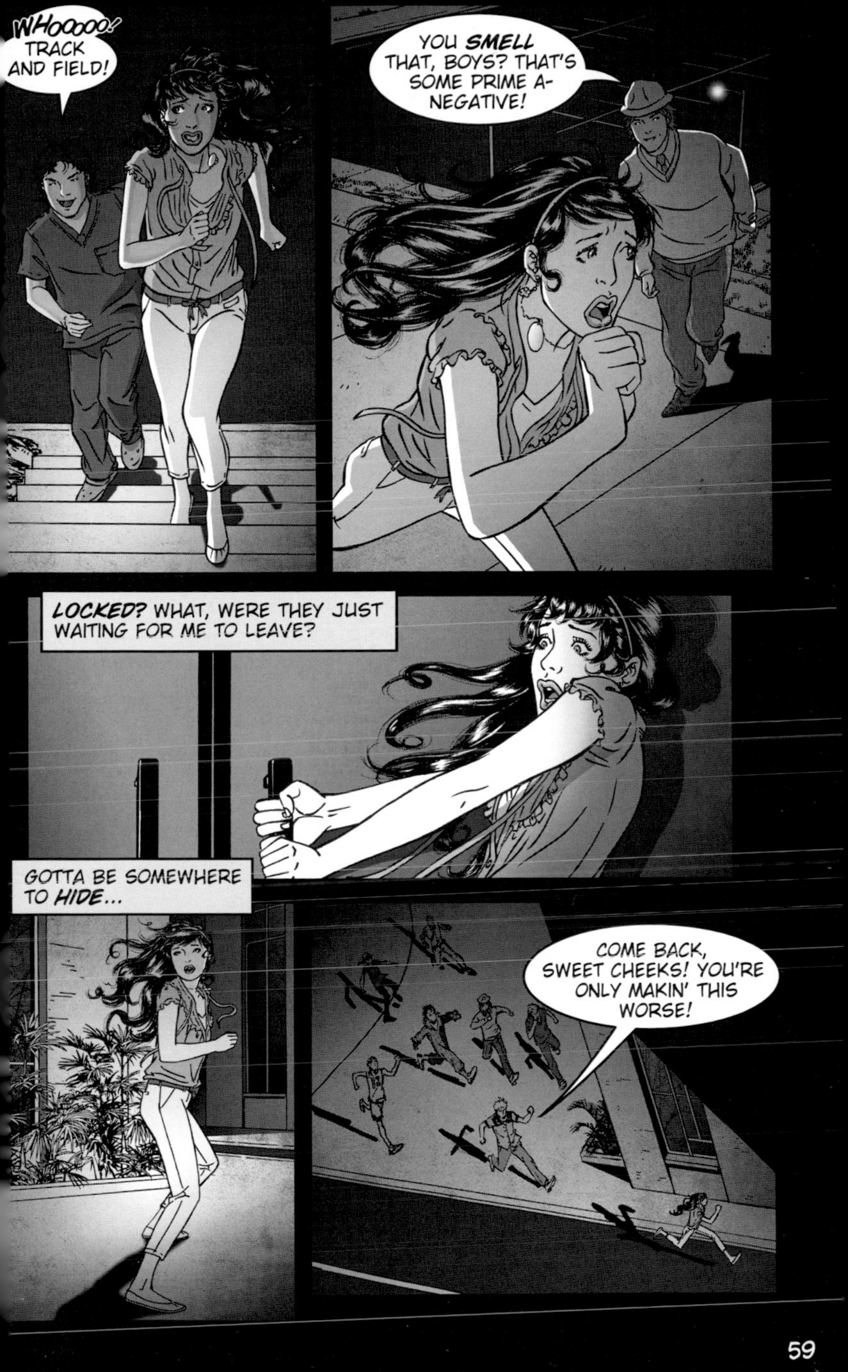
WHOOOOO! TRACK AND FIELD!
YOU SMELL THAT, BOYS? THAT'S SOME PRIME A-NEGATIVE!
LOCKED? WHAT, WERE THEY JUST WAITING FOR ME TO LEAVE?
GOTTA BE SOMEWHERE TO HIDE...
COME BACK, SWEET CHEEKS! YOU'RE ONLY MAKIN' THIS WORSE!

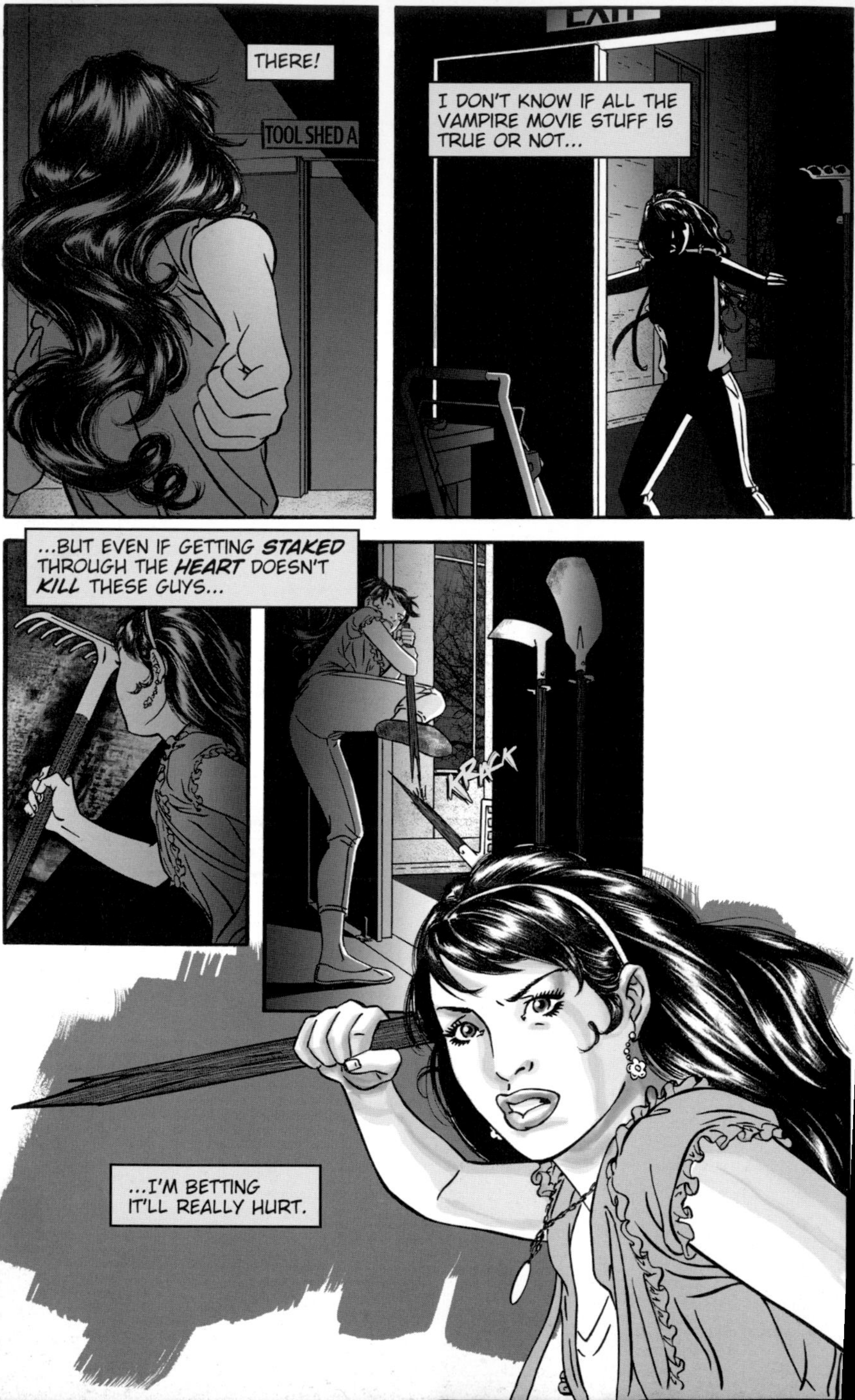
THERE!
TOOL SHED A
EXIT
I DON'T KNOW IF ALL THE VAMPIRE MOVIE STUFF IS TRUE OR NOT...
...BUT EVEN IF GETTING STAKED THROUGH THE HEART DOESN'T KILL THESE GUYS...
KRACK
...I'M BETTING IT'LL REALLY HURT.

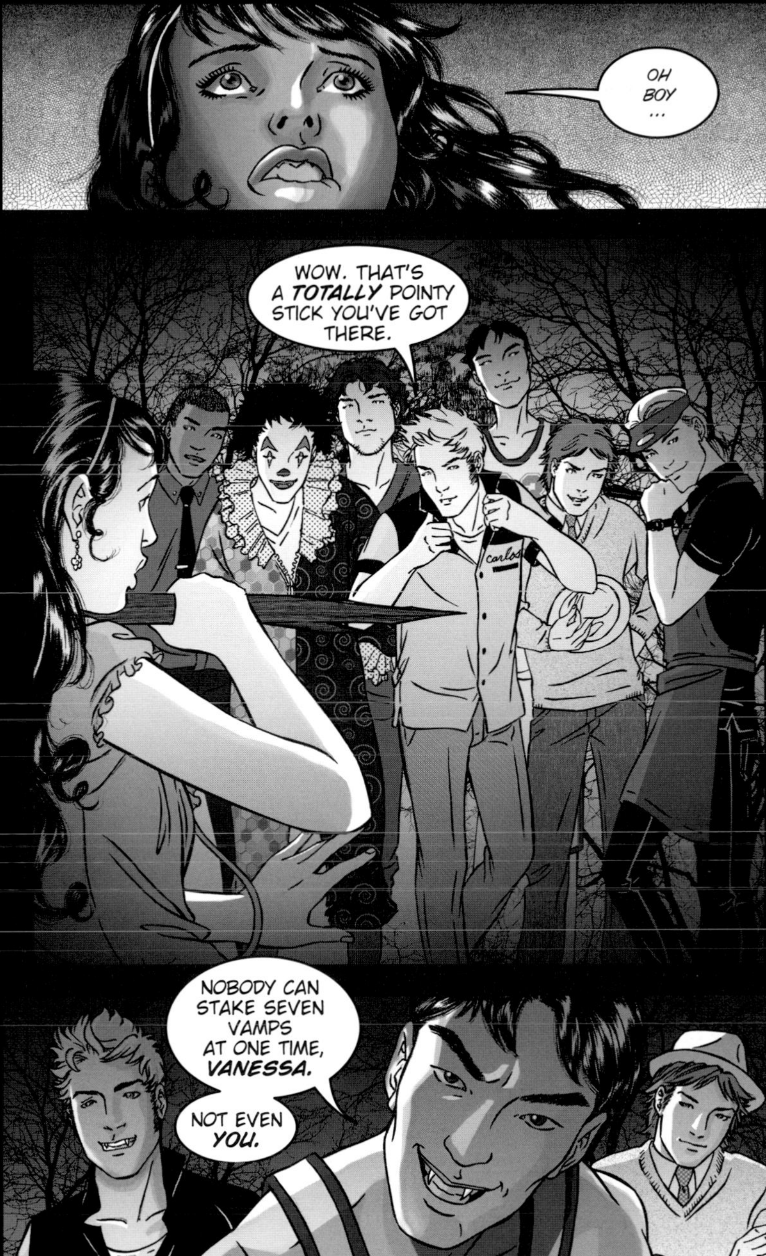

OH BOY ...
WOW. THAT'S A **TOTALLY** POINTY STICK YOU'VE GOT THERE.
carlos
NOBODY CAN STAKE SEVEN VAMPS AT ONE TIME, **VANESSA.**
NOT EVEN **YOU.**

Chapter 3
Painful Truths

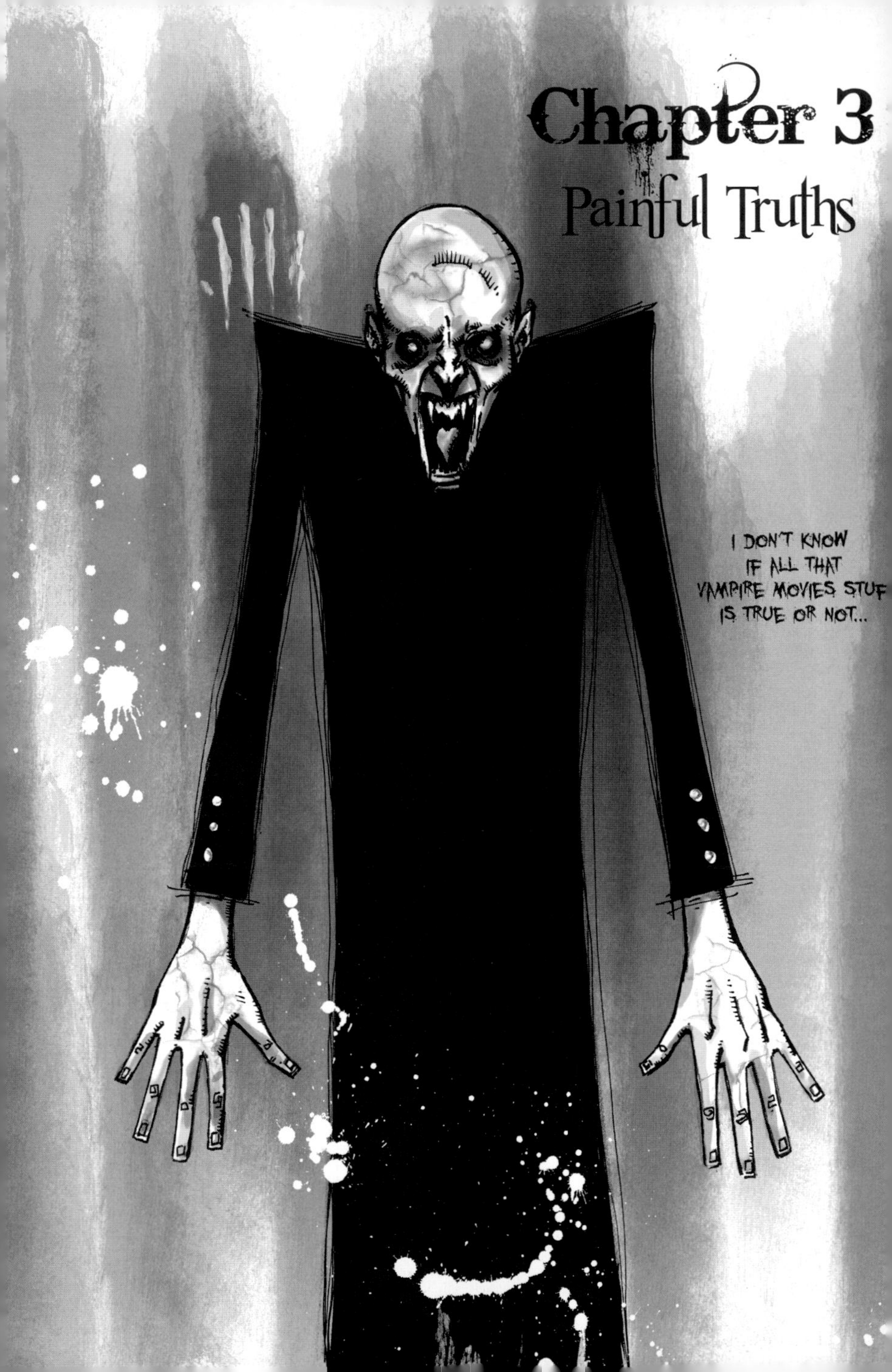
I DON'T KNOW IF ALL THAT VAMPIRE MOVIES STUF IS TRUE OR NOT...

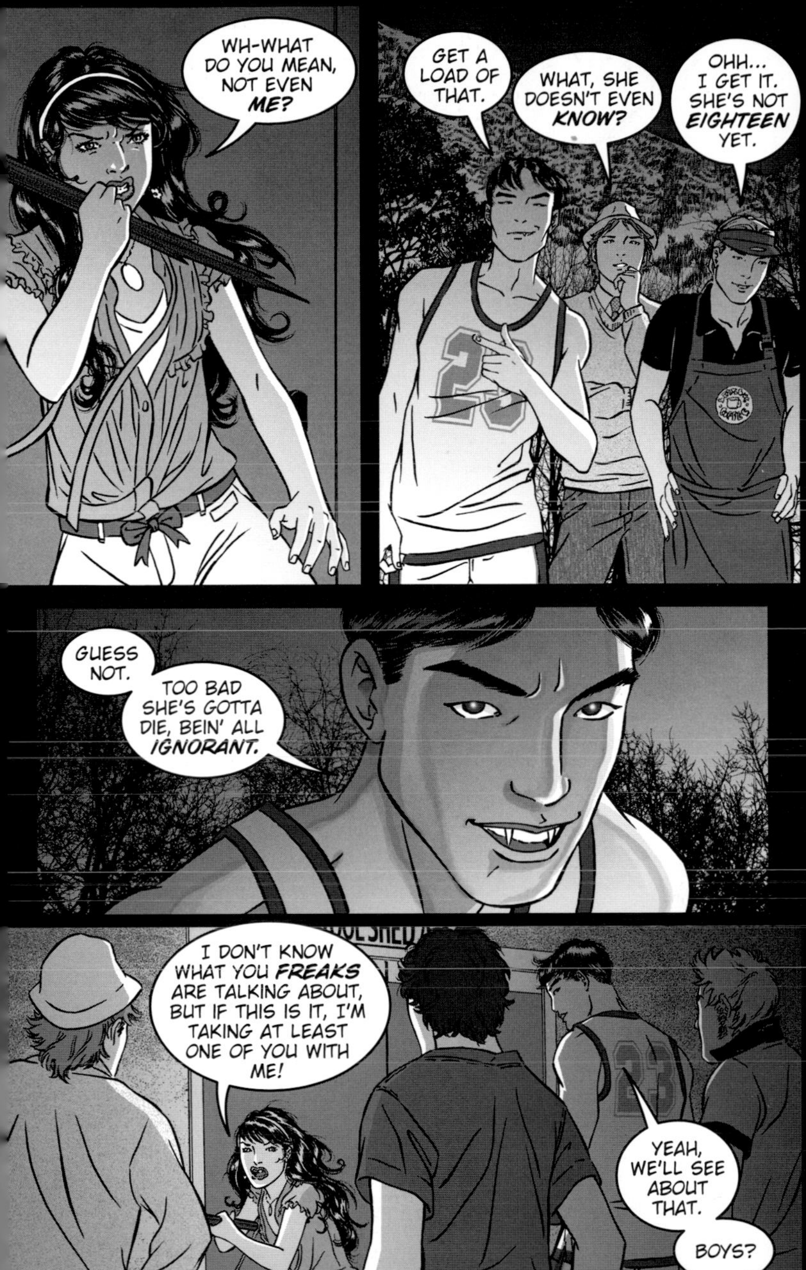
WH-WHAT DO YOU MEAN, NOT EVEN ME?
GET A LOAD OF THAT.
WHAT, SHE DOESN'T EVEN KNOW?
OHH... I GET IT. SHE'S NOT EIGHTEEN YET.
GUESS NOT.
TOO BAD SHE'S GOTTA DIE, BEIN' ALL IGNORANT.
I DON'T KNOW WHAT YOU FREAKS ARE TALKING ABOUT, BUT IF THIS IS IT, I'M TAKING AT LEAST ONE OF YOU WITH ME!
YEAH, WE'LL SEE ABOUT THAT.
BOYS?

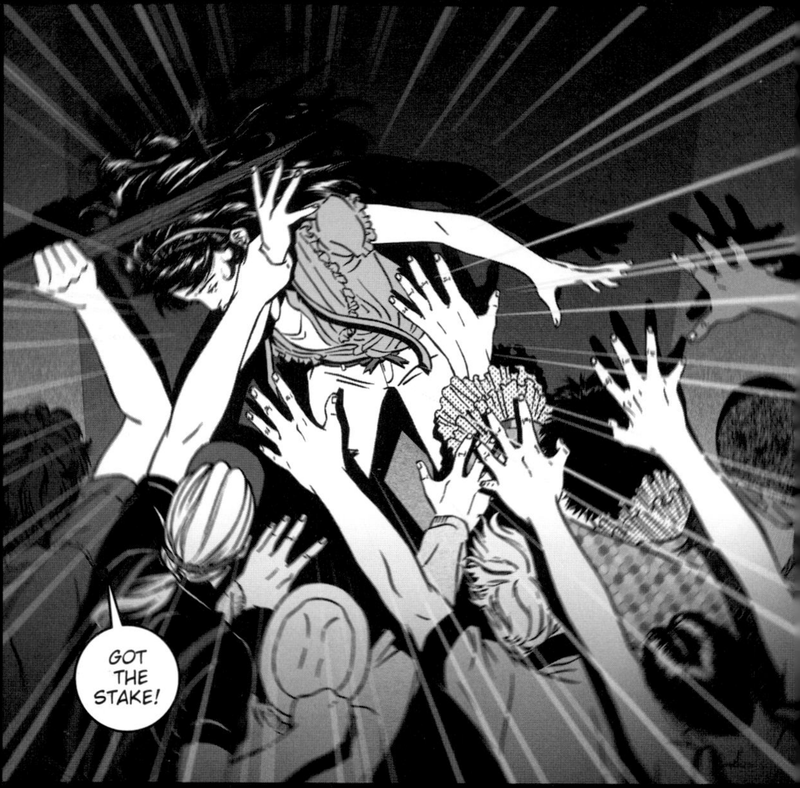
GOT THE STAKE!

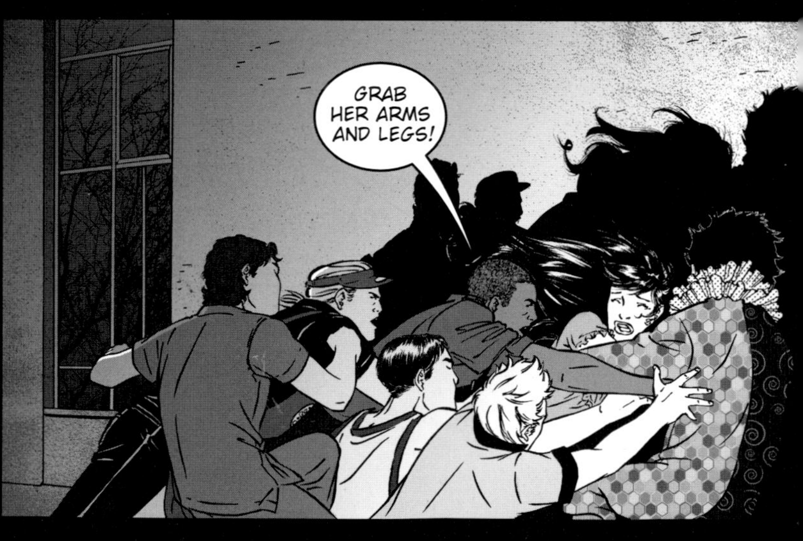
GRAB HER ARMS AND LEGS!

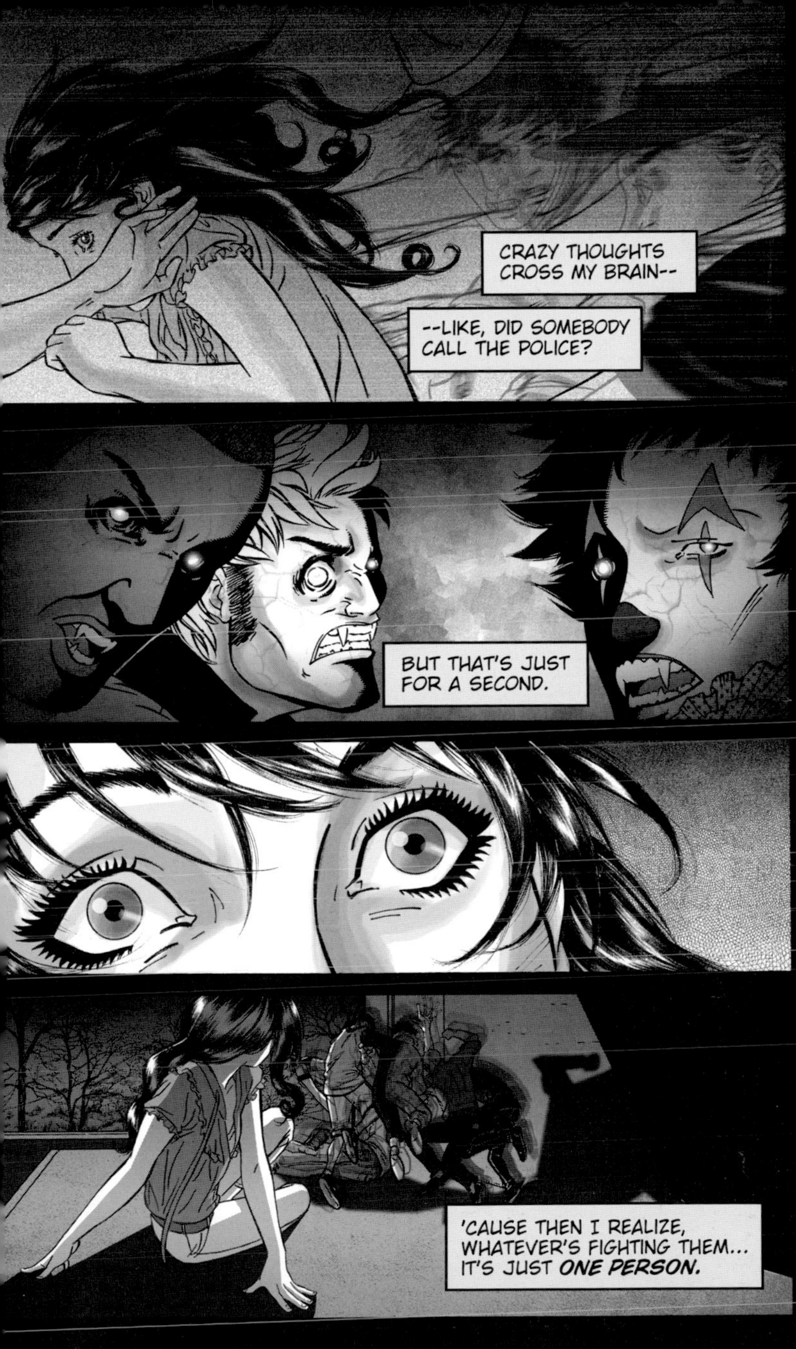
CRAZY THOUGHTS CROSS MY BRAIN--
--LIKE, DID SOMEBODY CALL THE POLICE?
BUT THAT'S JUST FOR A SECOND.
'CAUSE THEN I REALIZE, WHATEVER'S FIGHTING THEM... IT'S JUST ***ONE PERSON.***

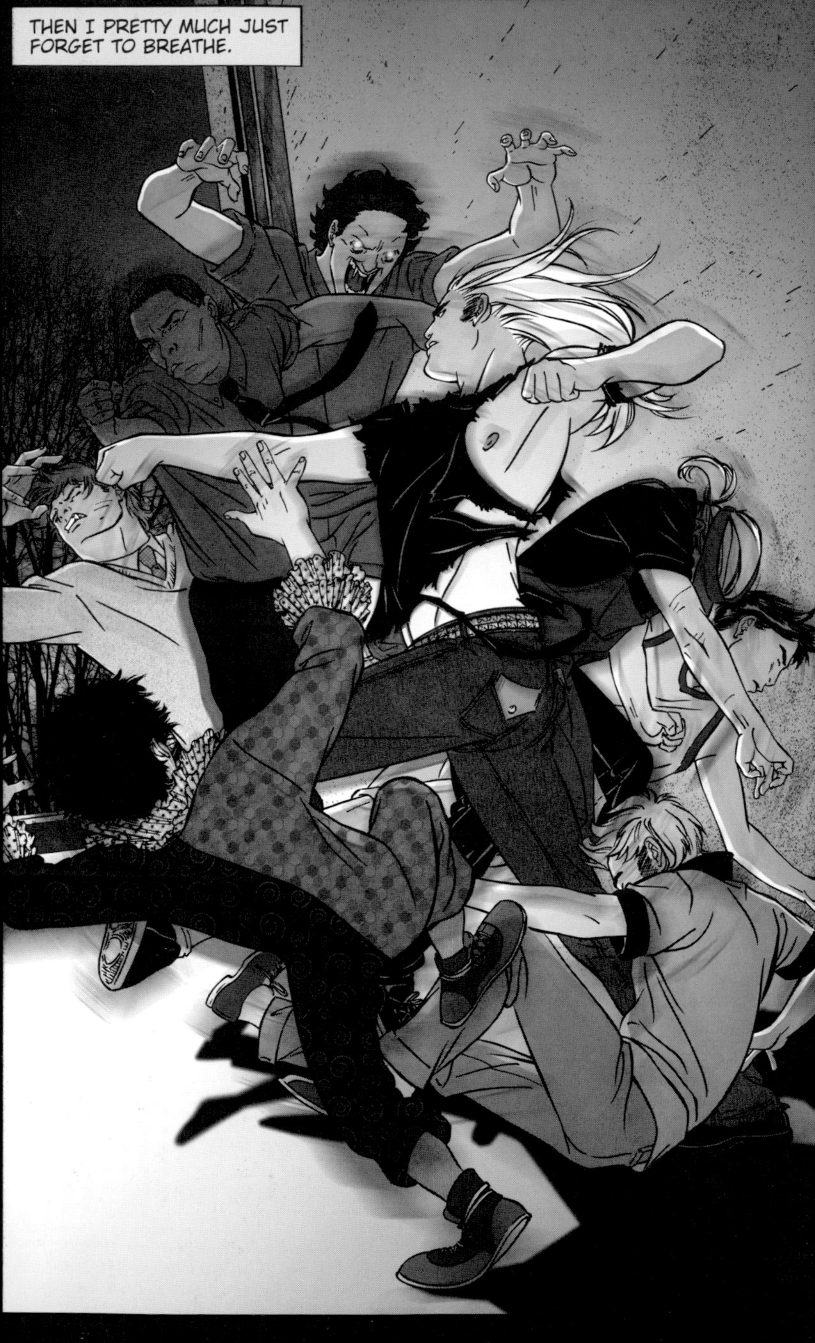
THEN I PRETTY MUCH JUST FORGET TO BREATHE.

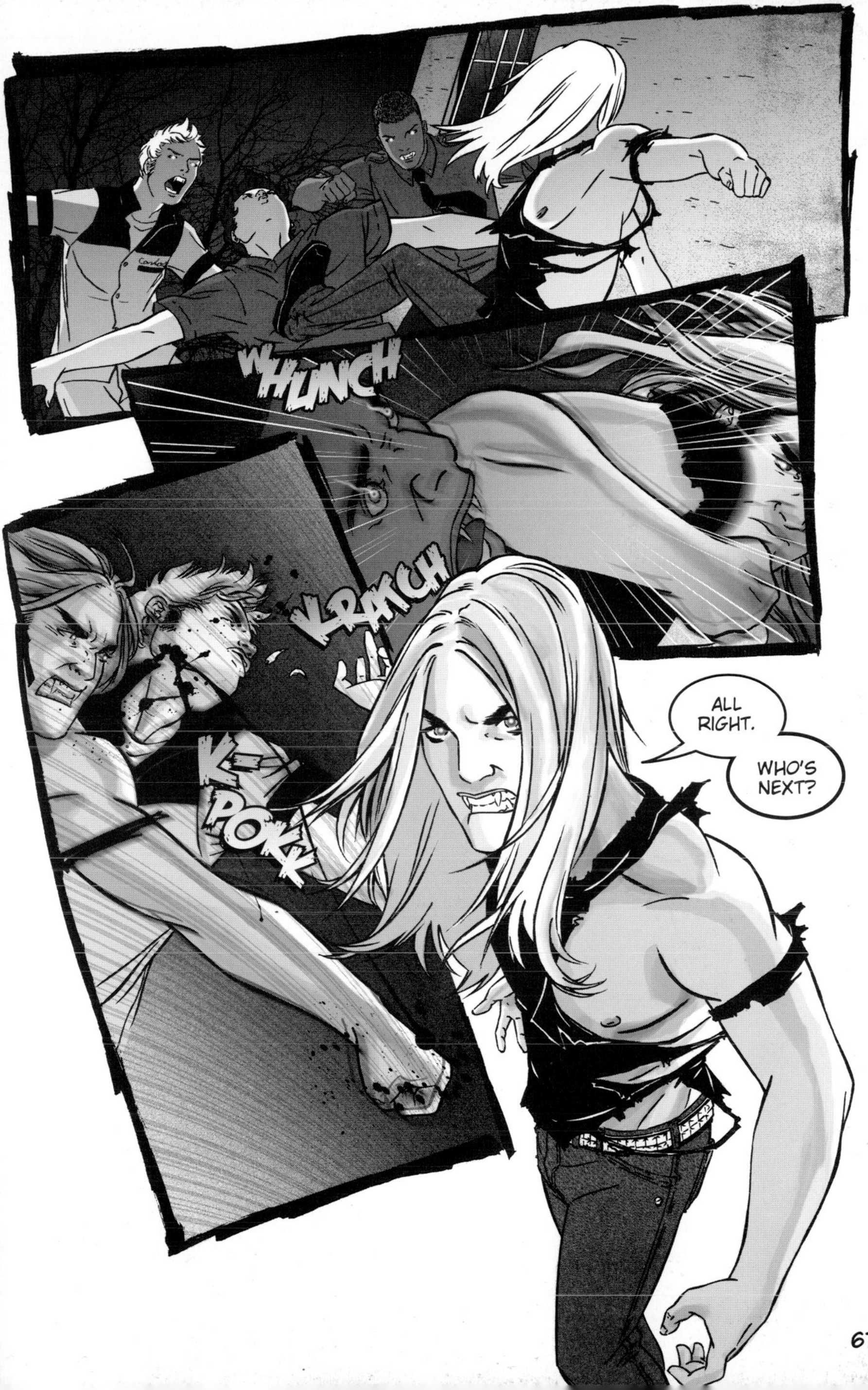
WHUNCH
KRACH
K-POKK
ALL RIGHT.
WHO'S NEXT?

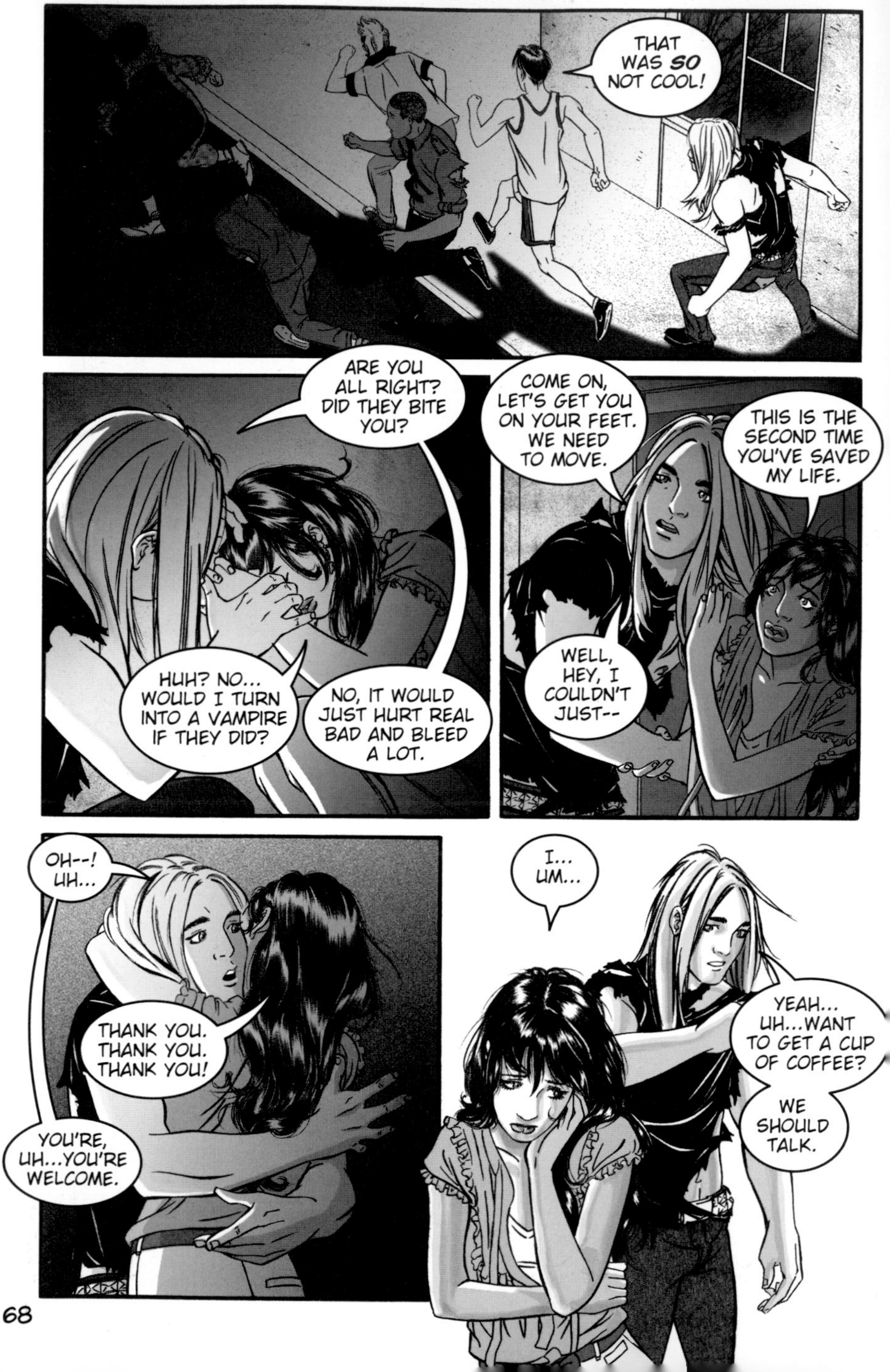
THAT WAS SO NOT COOL!
ARE YOU ALL RIGHT? DID THEY BITE YOU?
HUH? NO... WOULD I TURN INTO A VAMPIRE IF THEY DID?
NO, IT WOULD JUST HURT REAL BAD AND BLEED A LOT.
COME ON, LET'S GET YOU ON YOUR FEET. WE NEED TO MOVE.
THIS IS THE SECOND TIME YOU'VE SAVED MY LIFE.
WELL, HEY, I COULDN'T JUST--
OH--! UH...
THANK YOU. THANK YOU. THANK YOU!
YOU'RE, UH...YOU'RE WELCOME.
I... UM...
YEAH... UH...WANT TO GET A CUP OF COFFEE?
WE SHOULD TALK.

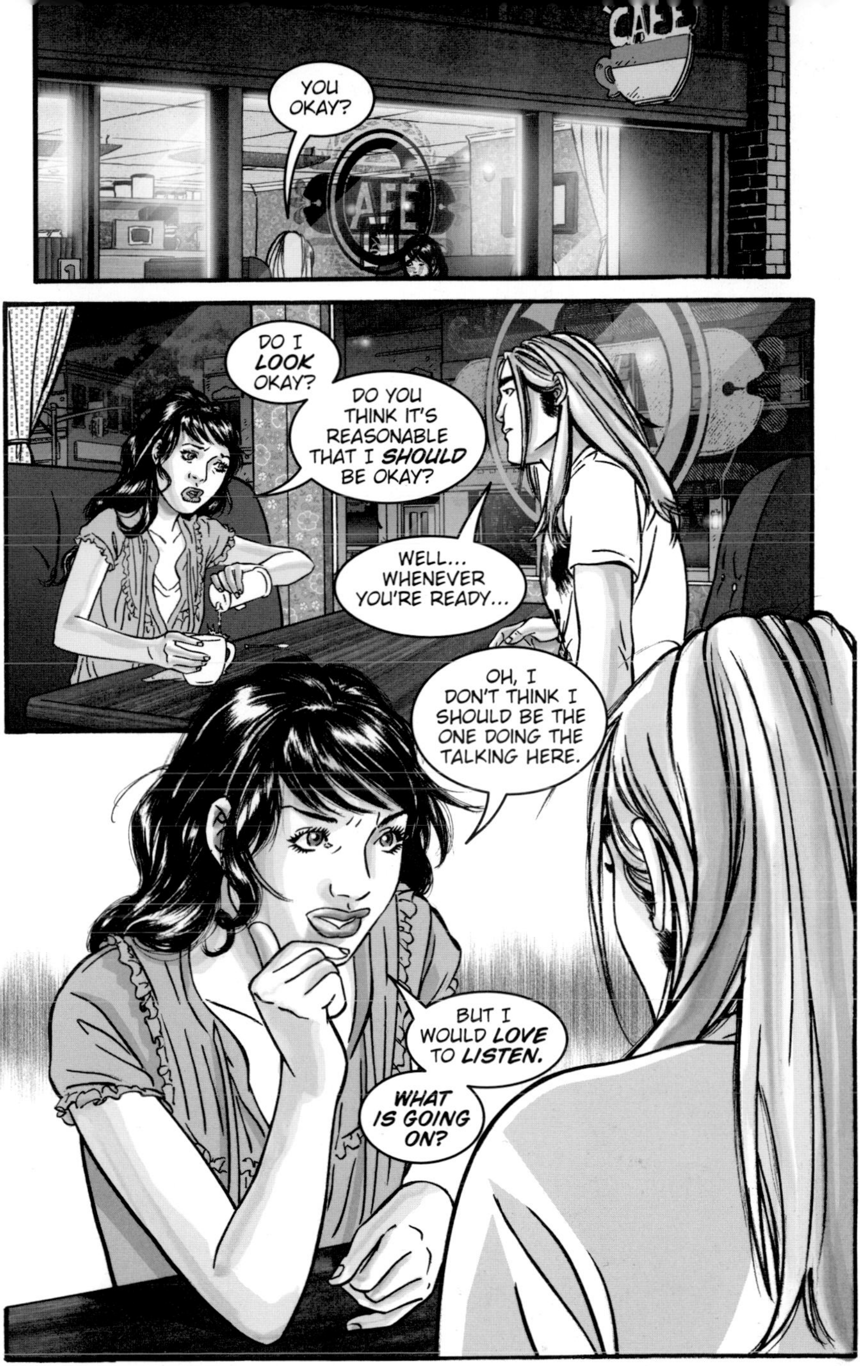
CAFE
YOU OKAY?
CAFE
DO I *LOOK* OKAY?
DO YOU THINK IT'S REASONABLE THAT I *SHOULD* BE OKAY?
WELL... WHENEVER YOU'RE READY...
OH, I DON'T THINK I SHOULD BE THE ONE DOING THE TALKING HERE.
BUT I WOULD *LOVE* TO *LISTEN.*
WHAT IS GOING ON?

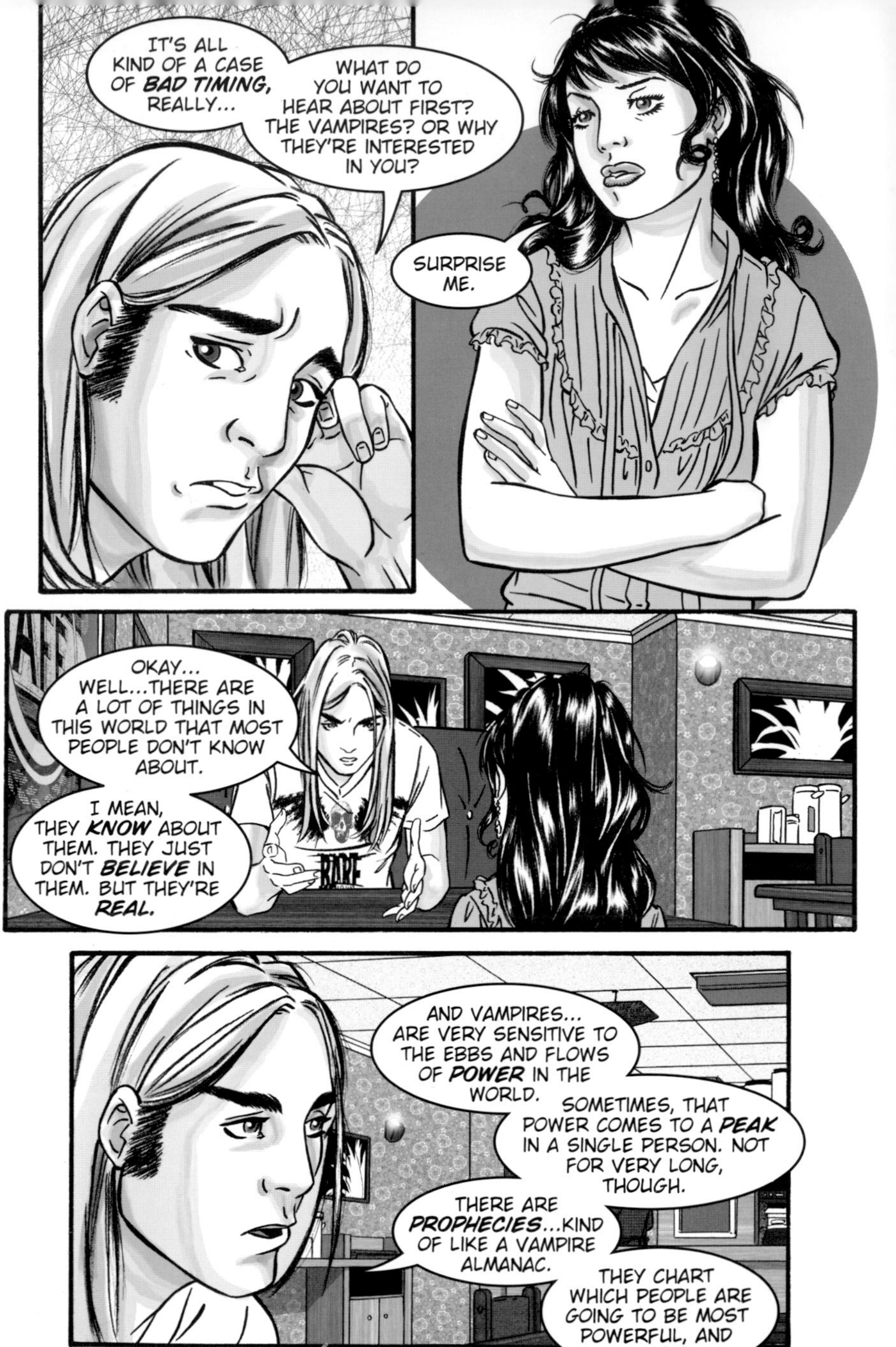
IT'S ALL KIND OF A CASE OF **BAD TIMING,** REALLY...
WHAT DO YOU WANT TO HEAR ABOUT FIRST? THE VAMPIRES? OR WHY THEY'RE INTERESTED IN YOU?
SURPRISE ME.
OKAY... WELL...THERE ARE A LOT OF THINGS IN THIS WORLD THAT MOST PEOPLE DON'T KNOW ABOUT.
I MEAN, THEY **KNOW** ABOUT THEM. THEY JUST DON'T **BELIEVE** IN THEM. BUT THEY'RE **REAL.**
AND VAMPIRES... ARE VERY SENSITIVE TO THE EBBS AND FLOWS OF **POWER** IN THE WORLD.
SOMETIMES, THAT POWER COMES TO A **PEAK** IN A SINGLE PERSON. NOT FOR VERY LONG, THOUGH.
THERE ARE **PROPHECIES**...KIND OF LIKE A VAMPIRE ALMANAC.
THEY CHART WHICH PEOPLE ARE GOING TO BE MOST POWERFUL, AND **WHEN.**

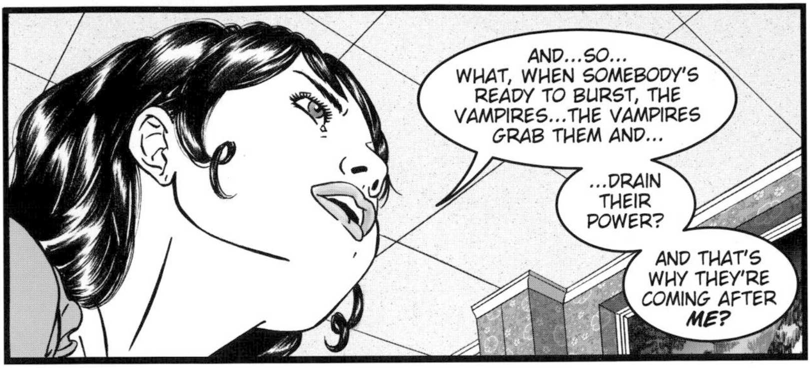
AND...SO...
WHAT, WHEN SOMEBODY'S READY TO BURST, THE VAMPIRES...THE VAMPIRES GRAB THEM AND...
...DRAIN THEIR POWER?
AND THAT'S WHY THEY'RE COMING AFTER ME?

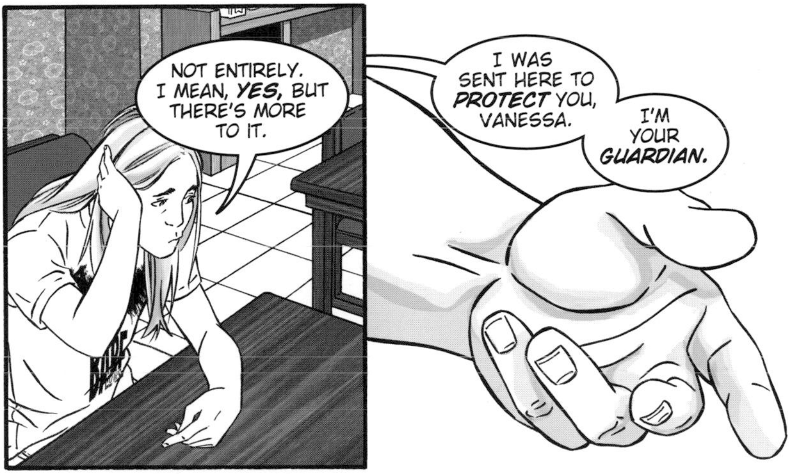
NOT ENTIRELY. I MEAN, YES, BUT THERE'S MORE TO IT.
I WAS SENT HERE TO PROTECT YOU, VANESSA.
I'M YOUR GUARDIAN.

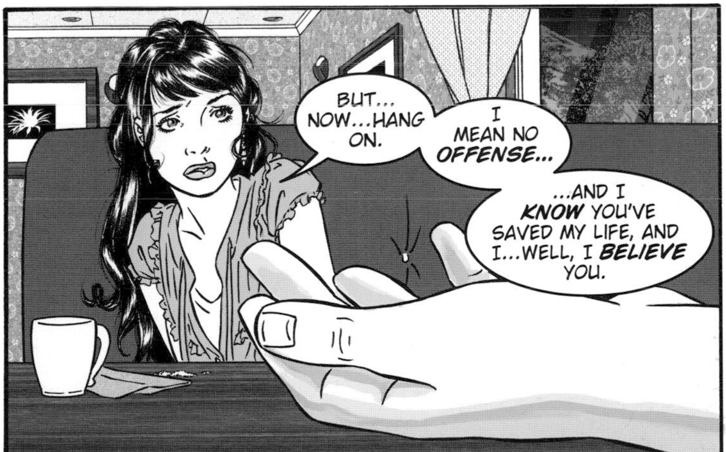
BUT... NOW...HANG ON.
I MEAN NO OFFENSE...
...AND I KNOW YOU'VE SAVED MY LIFE, AND I...WELL, I BELIEVE YOU.

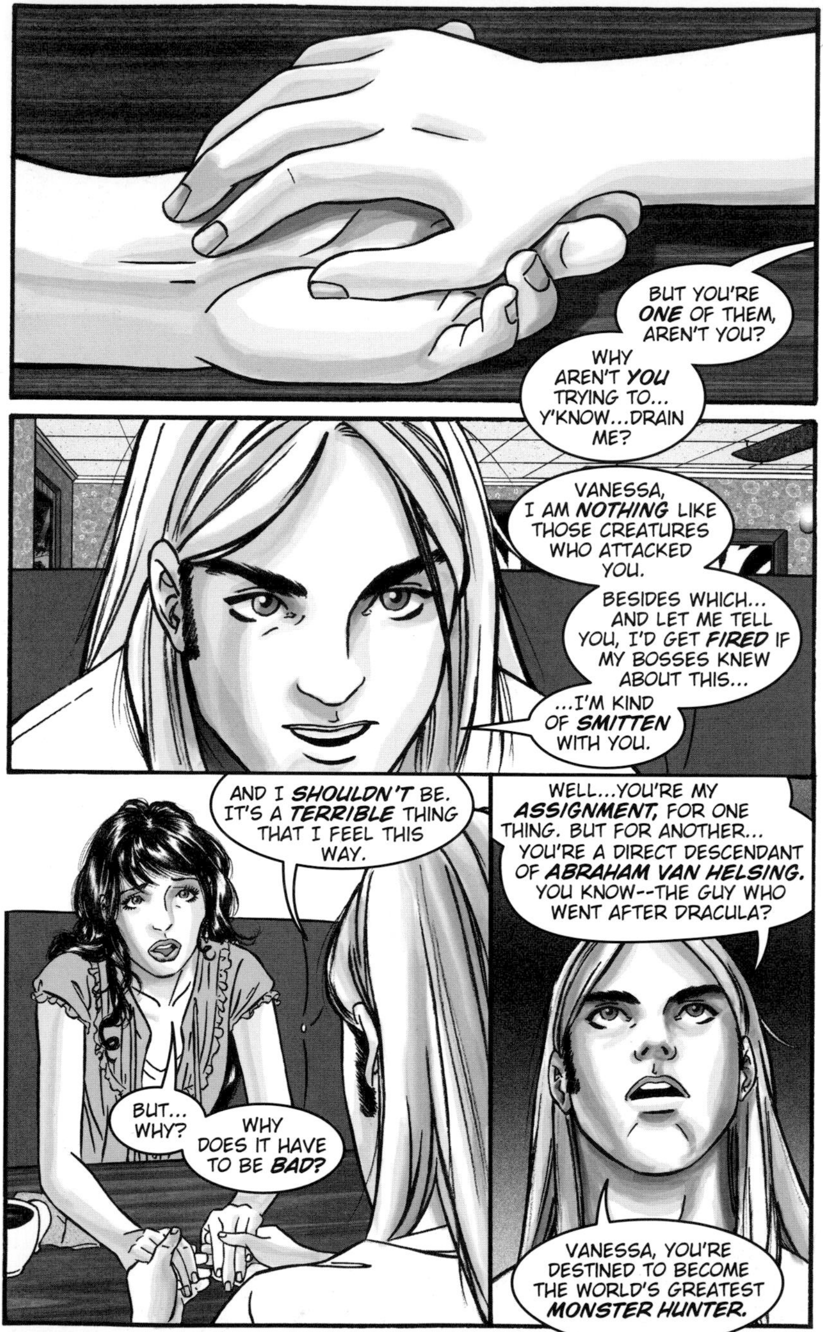
BUT YOU'RE ONE OF THEM, AREN'T YOU?
WHY AREN'T YOU TRYING TO... Y'KNOW...DRAIN ME?
VANESSA, I AM NOTHING LIKE THOSE CREATURES WHO ATTACKED YOU.
BESIDES WHICH... AND LET ME TELL YOU, I'D GET FIRED IF MY BOSSES KNEW ABOUT THIS...
...I'M KIND OF SMITTEN WITH YOU.
AND I SHOULDN'T BE. IT'S A TERRIBLE THING THAT I FEEL THIS WAY.
BUT... WHY?
WHY DOES IT HAVE TO BE BAD?
WELL...YOU'RE MY ASSIGNMENT, FOR ONE THING. BUT FOR ANOTHER... YOU'RE A DIRECT DESCENDANT OF ABRAHAM VAN HELSING. YOU KNOW--THE GUY WHO WENT AFTER DRACULA?
VANESSA, YOU'RE DESTINED TO BECOME THE WORLD'S GREATEST MONSTER HUNTER.

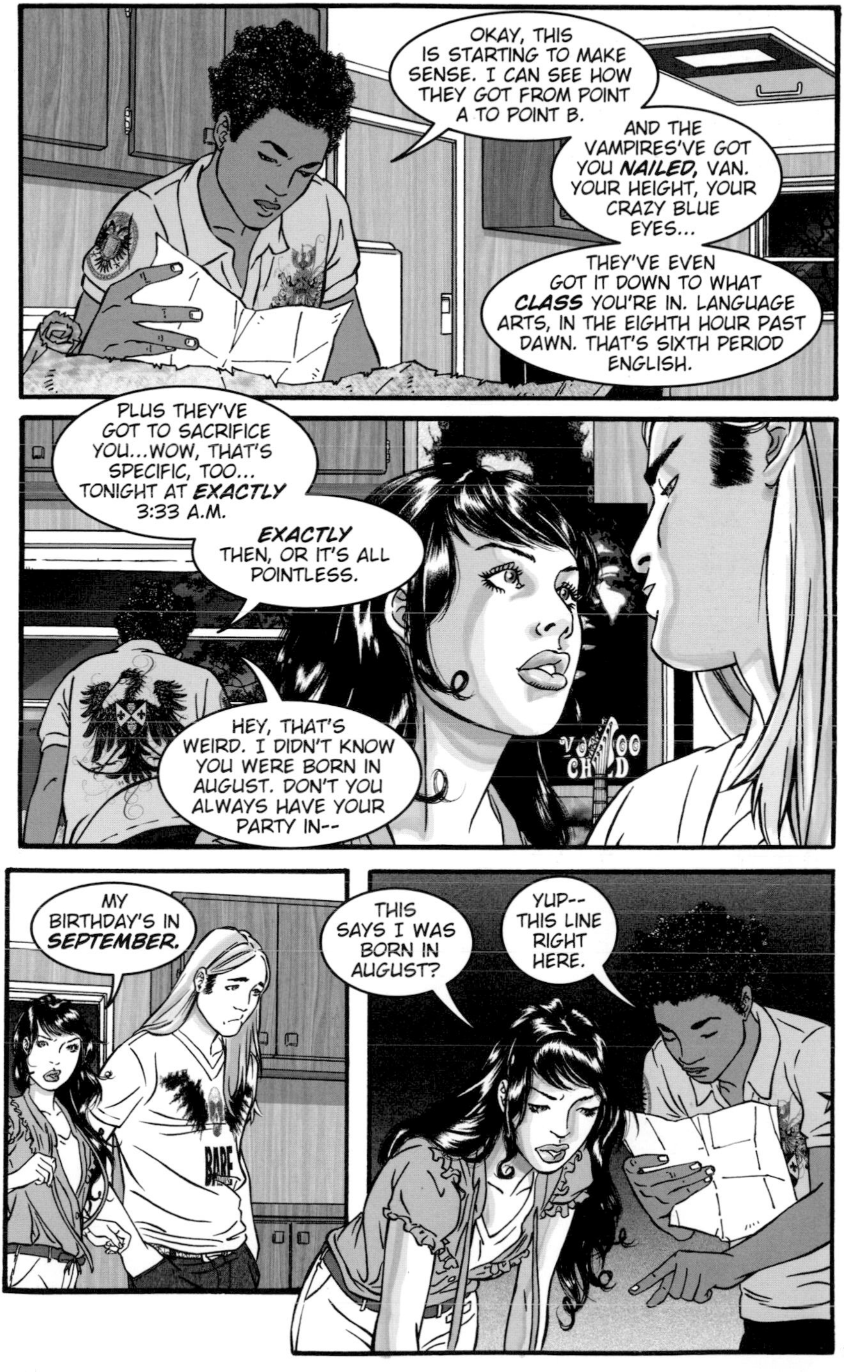
OKAY, THIS IS STARTING TO MAKE SENSE. I CAN SEE HOW THEY GOT FROM POINT A TO POINT B.
AND THE VAMPIRES'VE GOT YOU NAILED, VAN. YOUR HEIGHT, YOUR CRAZY BLUE EYES...
THEY'VE EVEN GOT IT DOWN TO WHAT CLASS YOU'RE IN. LANGUAGE ARTS, IN THE EIGHTH HOUR PAST DAWN. THAT'S SIXTH PERIOD ENGLISH.
PLUS THEY'VE GOT TO SACRIFICE YOU...WOW, THAT'S SPECIFIC, TOO... TONIGHT AT EXACTLY 3:33 A.M.
EXACTLY THEN, OR IT'S ALL POINTLESS.
HEY, THAT'S WEIRD. I DIDN'T KNOW YOU WERE BORN IN AUGUST. DON'T YOU ALWAYS HAVE YOUR PARTY IN--
MY BIRTHDAY'S IN SEPTEMBER.
THIS SAYS I WAS BORN IN AUGUST?
YUP-- THIS LINE RIGHT HERE.

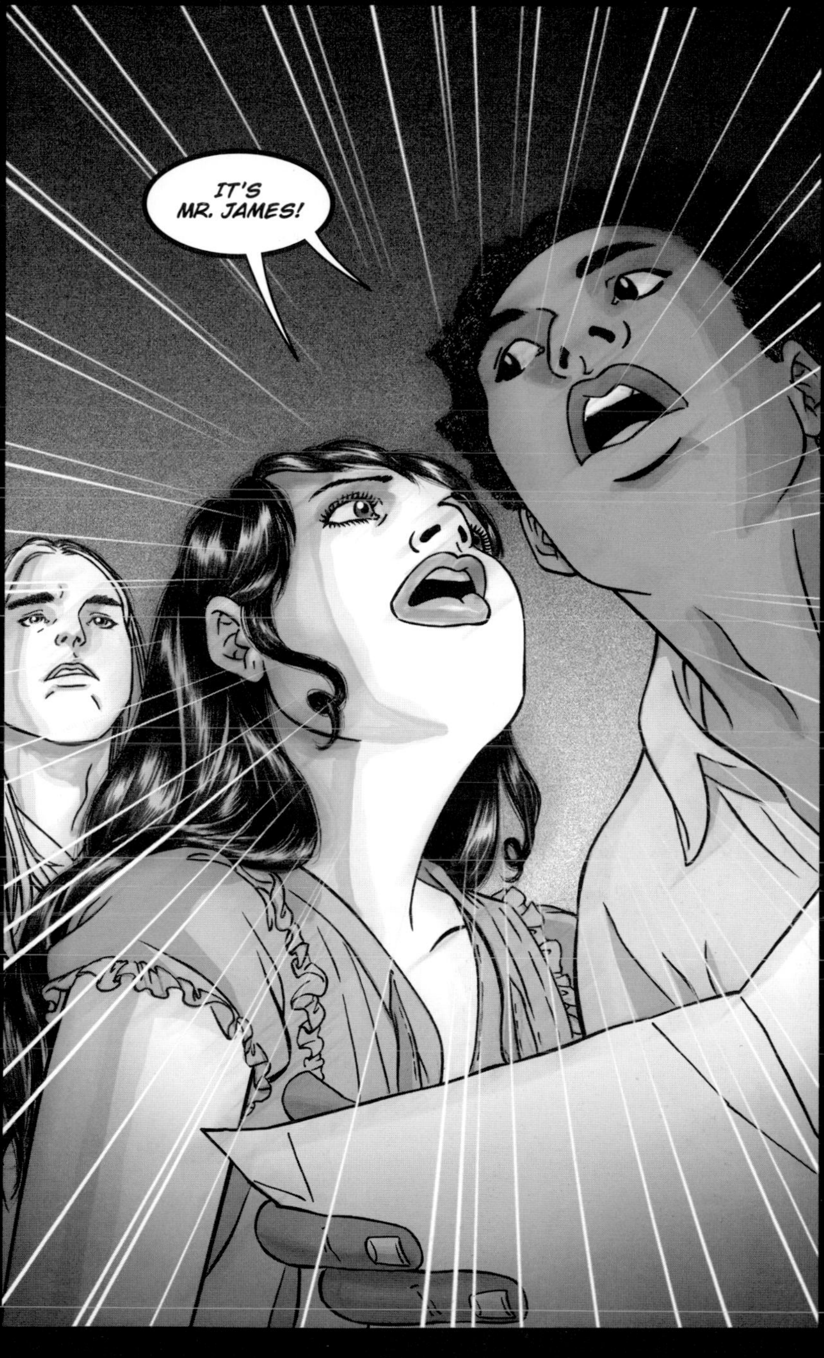
IT'S MR. JAMES!

81

84

86

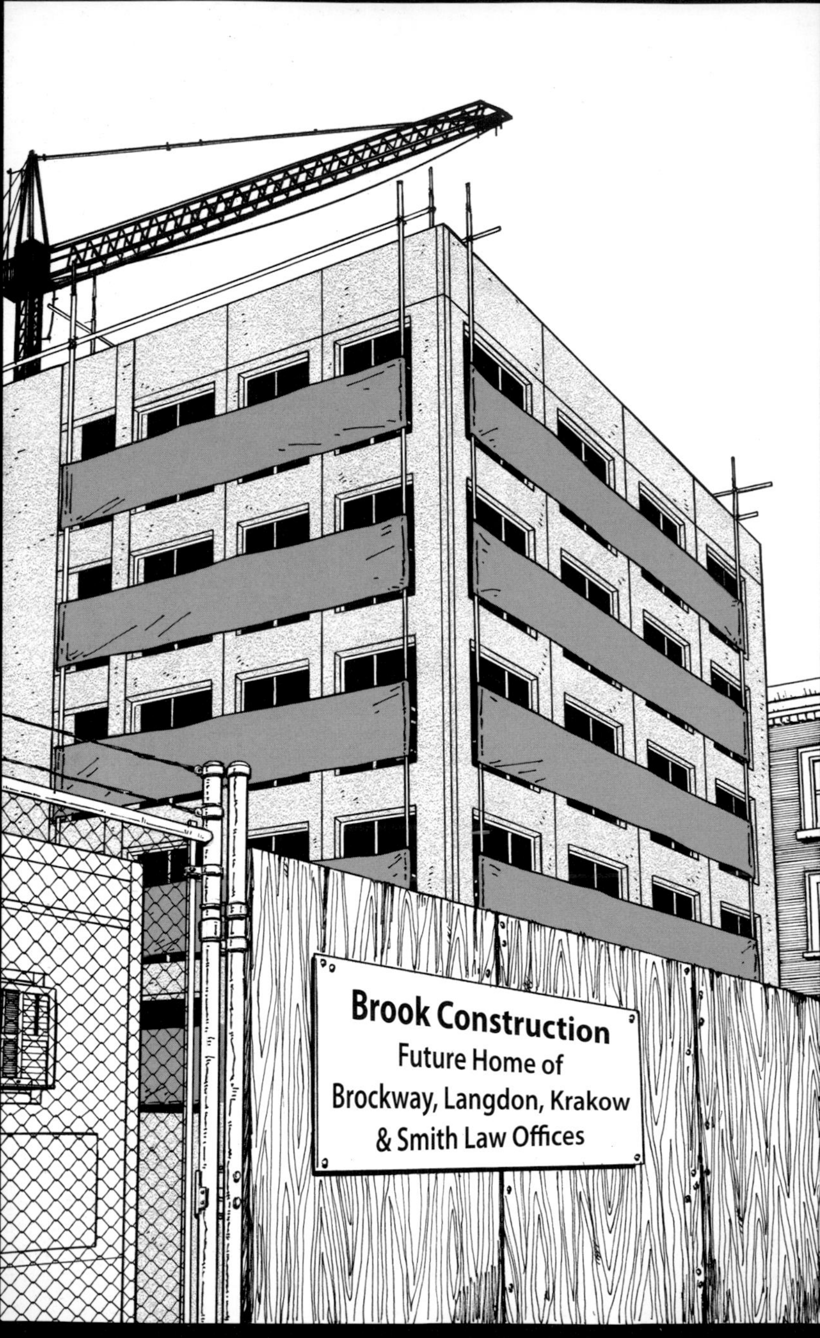
Brook Construction
Future Home of
Brockway, Langdon, Krakow
& Smith Law Offices

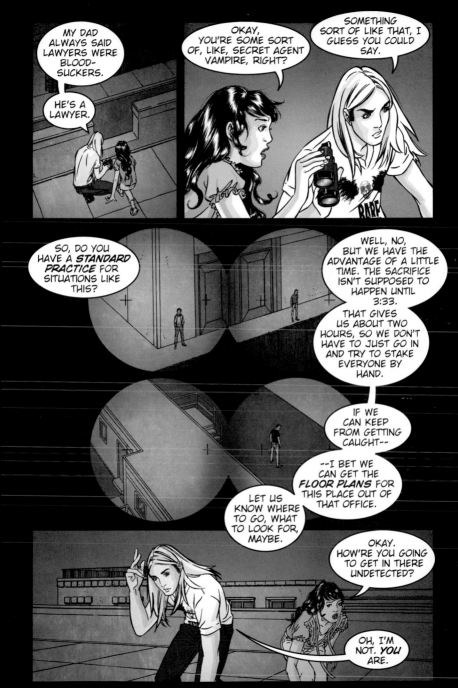

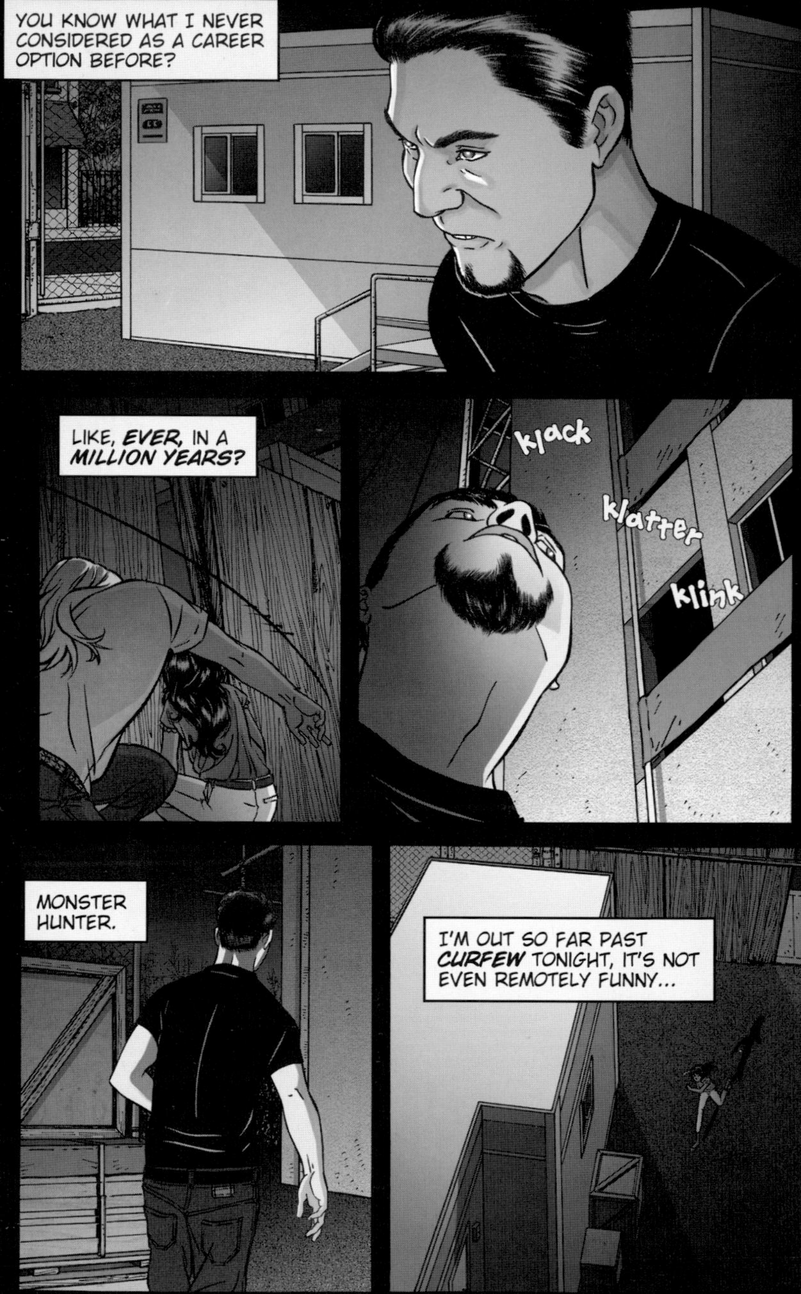
YOU KNOW WHAT I NEVER CONSIDERED AS A CAREER OPTION BEFORE?
LIKE, EVER, IN A MILLION YEARS?
klack
klatter
klink
MONSTER HUNTER.
I'M OUT SO FAR PAST CURFEW TONIGHT, IT'S NOT EVEN REMOTELY FUNNY...

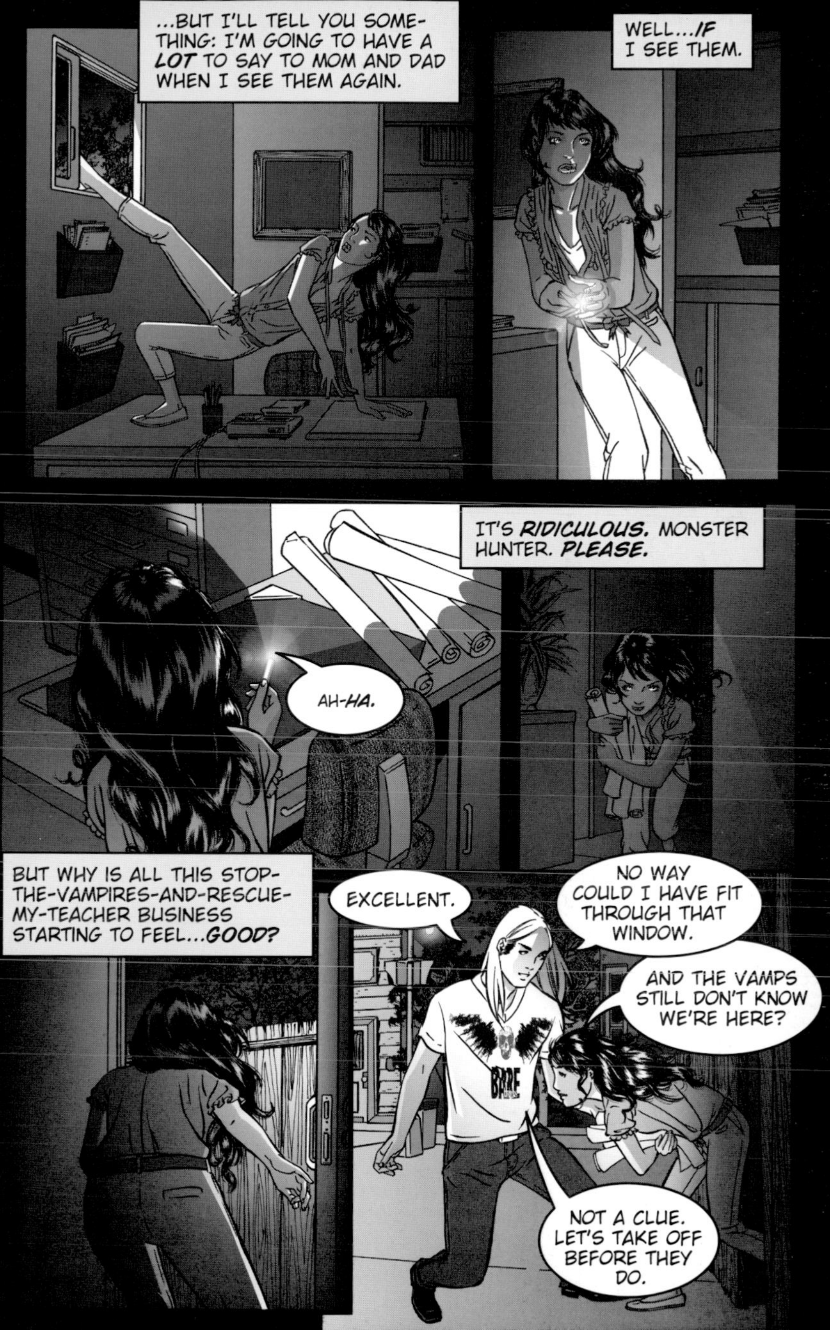
...BUT I'LL TELL YOU SOMETHING: I'M GOING TO HAVE A LOT TO SAY TO MOM AND DAD WHEN I SEE THEM AGAIN.
WELL...IF I SEE THEM.
IT'S RIDICULOUS. MONSTER HUNTER. PLEASE.
AH-HA.
BUT WHY IS ALL THIS STOP-THE-VAMPIRES-AND-RESCUE-MY-TEACHER BUSINESS STARTING TO FEEL...GOOD?
EXCELLENT.
NO WAY COULD I HAVE FIT THROUGH THAT WINDOW.
AND THE VAMPS STILL DON'T KNOW WE'RE HERE?
NOT A CLUE. LET'S TAKE OFF BEFORE THEY DO.

Chapter 4
Compatibility Issues

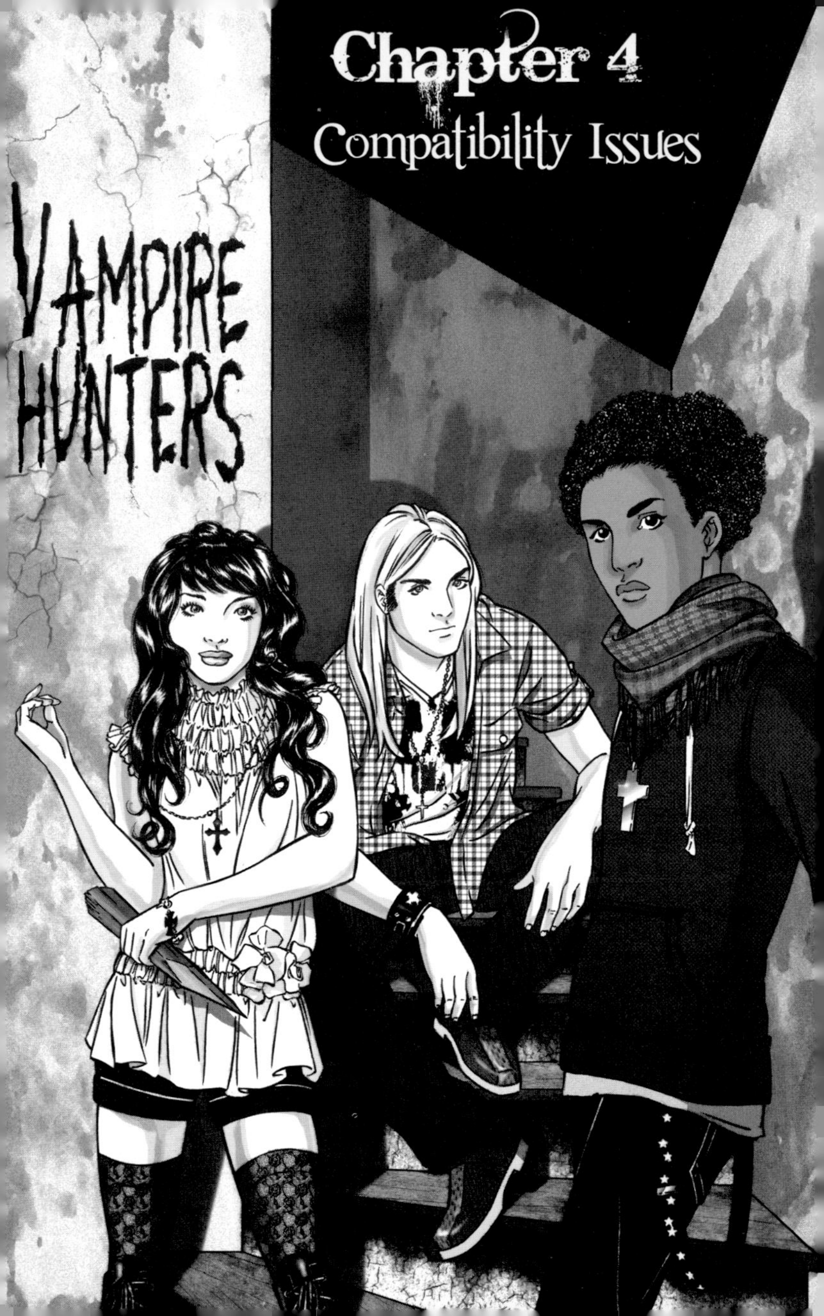
VAMPIRE HUNTERS

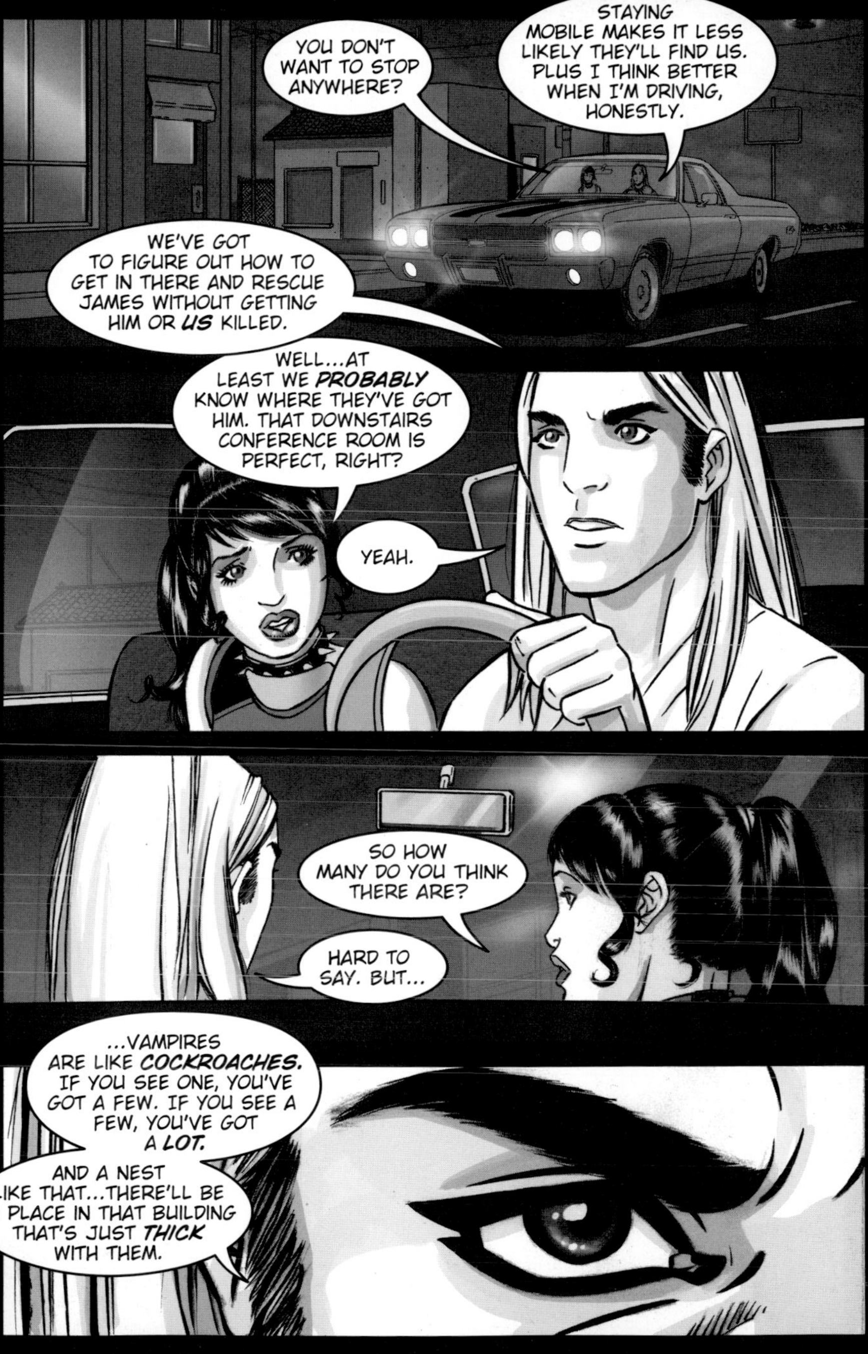
YOU DON'T WANT TO STOP ANYWHERE?
STAYING MOBILE MAKES IT LESS LIKELY THEY'LL FIND US. PLUS I THINK BETTER WHEN I'M DRIVING, HONESTLY.
WE'VE GOT TO FIGURE OUT HOW TO GET IN THERE AND RESCUE JAMES WITHOUT GETTING HIM OR *US* KILLED.
WELL...AT LEAST WE *PROBABLY* KNOW WHERE THEY'VE GOT HIM. THAT DOWNSTAIRS CONFERENCE ROOM IS PERFECT, RIGHT?
YEAH.
SO HOW MANY DO YOU THINK THERE ARE?
HARD TO SAY. BUT...
...VAMPIRES ARE LIKE *COCKROACHES.* IF YOU SEE ONE, YOU'VE GOT A FEW. IF YOU SEE A FEW, YOU'VE GOT A *LOT.*
AND A NEST LIKE THAT...THERE'LL BE A PLACE IN THAT BUILDING THAT'S JUST *THICK* WITH THEM.

95

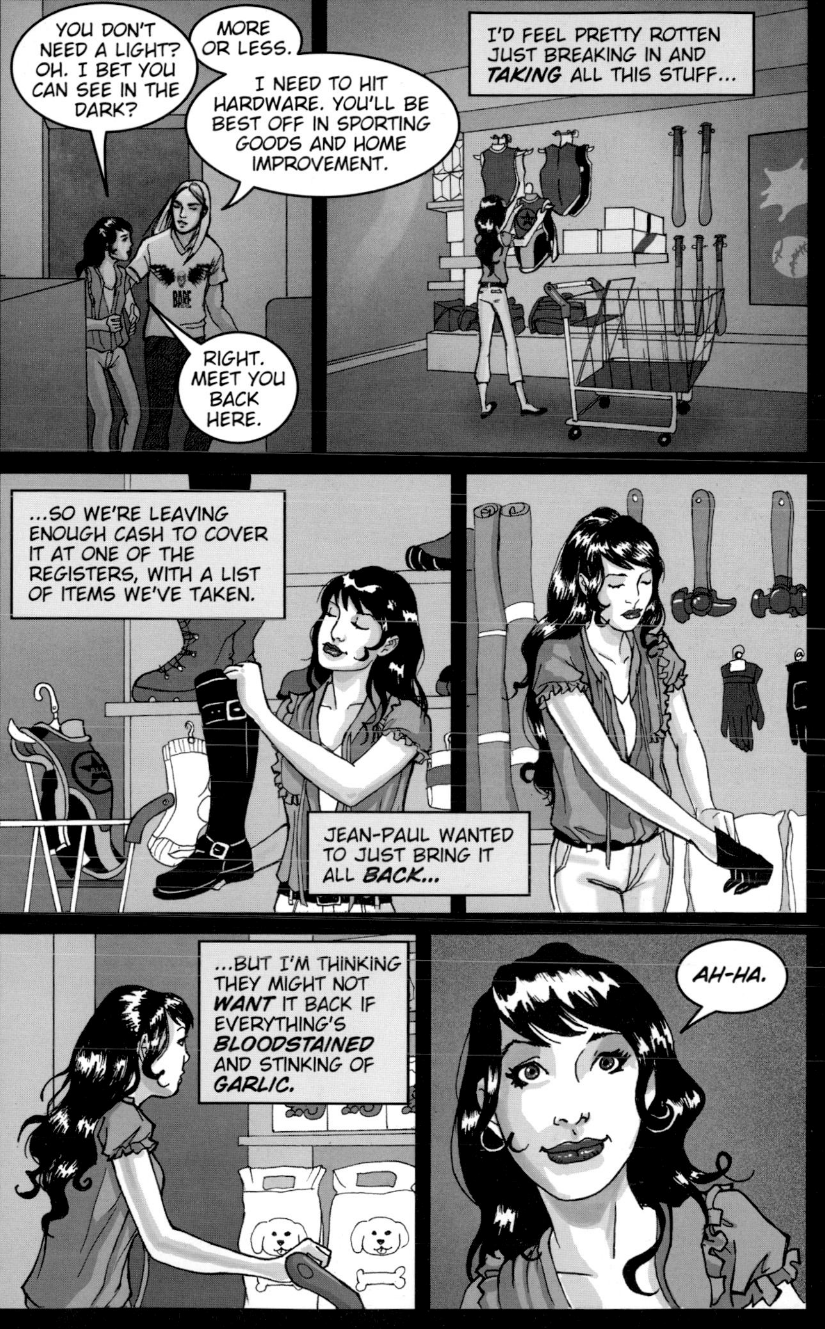

YOU DON'T NEED A LIGHT? OH. I BET YOU CAN SEE IN THE DARK?
MORE OR LESS.
I NEED TO HIT HARDWARE. YOU'LL BE BEST OFF IN SPORTING GOODS AND HOME IMPROVEMENT.
RIGHT. MEET YOU BACK HERE.
I'D FEEL PRETTY ROTTEN JUST BREAKING IN AND TAKING ALL THIS STUFF...
...SO WE'RE LEAVING ENOUGH CASH TO COVER IT AT ONE OF THE REGISTERS, WITH A LIST OF ITEMS WE'VE TAKEN.
JEAN-PAUL WANTED TO JUST BRING IT ALL BACK...
...BUT I'M THINKING THEY MIGHT NOT WANT IT BACK IF EVERYTHING'S BLOODSTAINED AND STINKING OF GARLIC.
AH-HA.

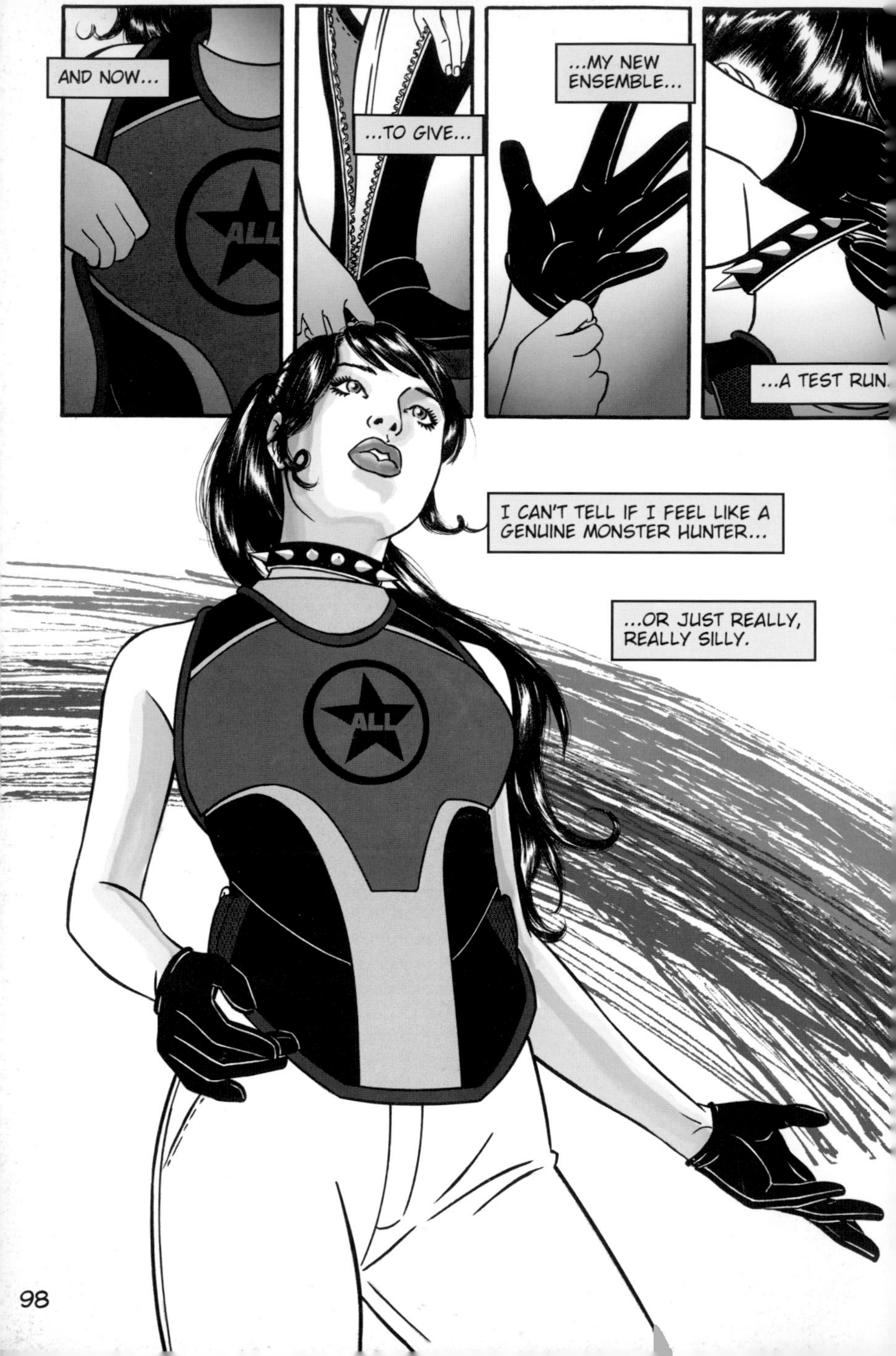
AND NOW...
...TO GIVE...
...MY NEW ENSEMBLE...
...A TEST RUN.
I CAN'T TELL IF I FEEL LIKE A GENUINE MONSTER HUNTER...
...OR JUST REALLY, REALLY SILLY.

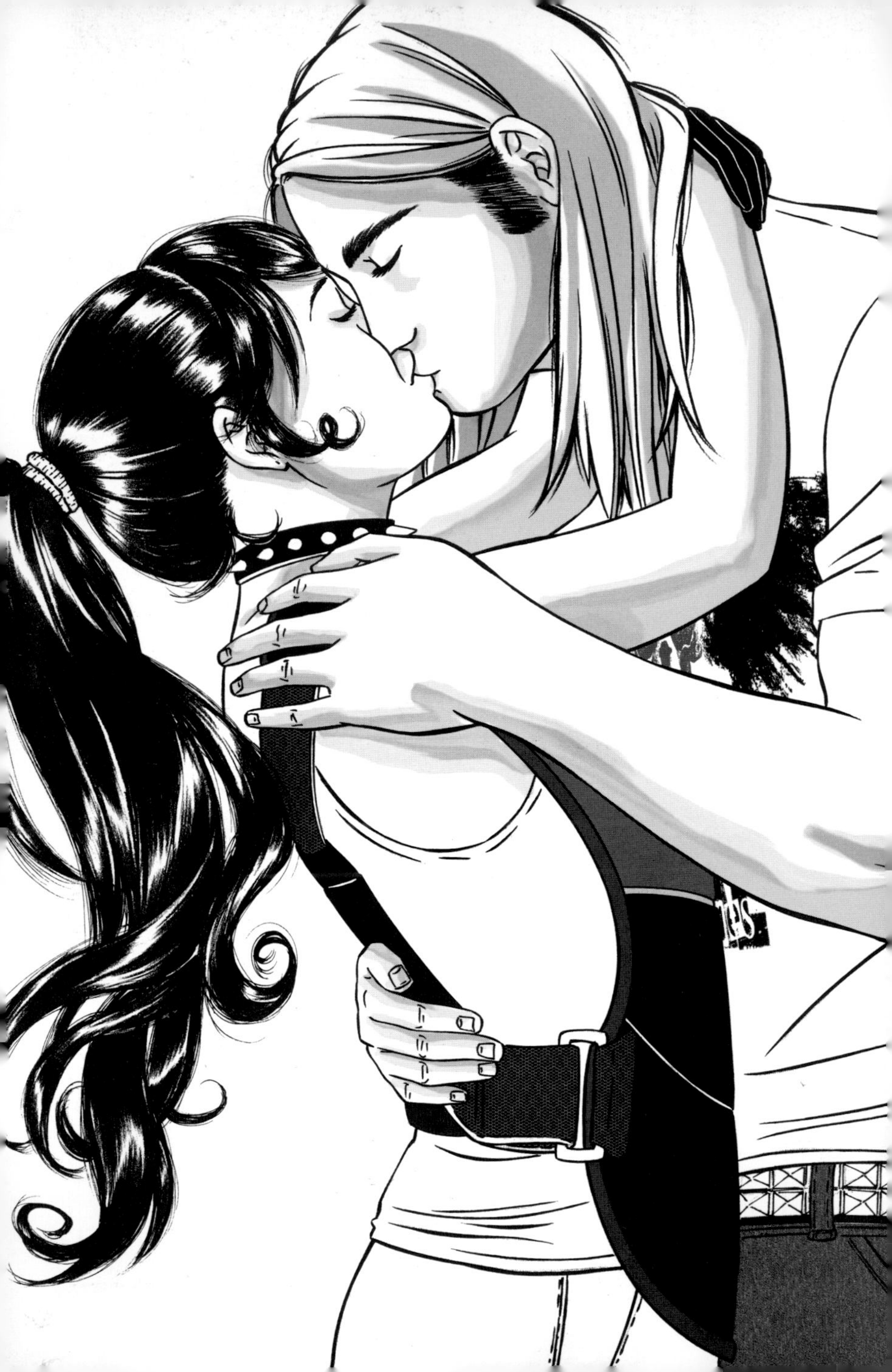

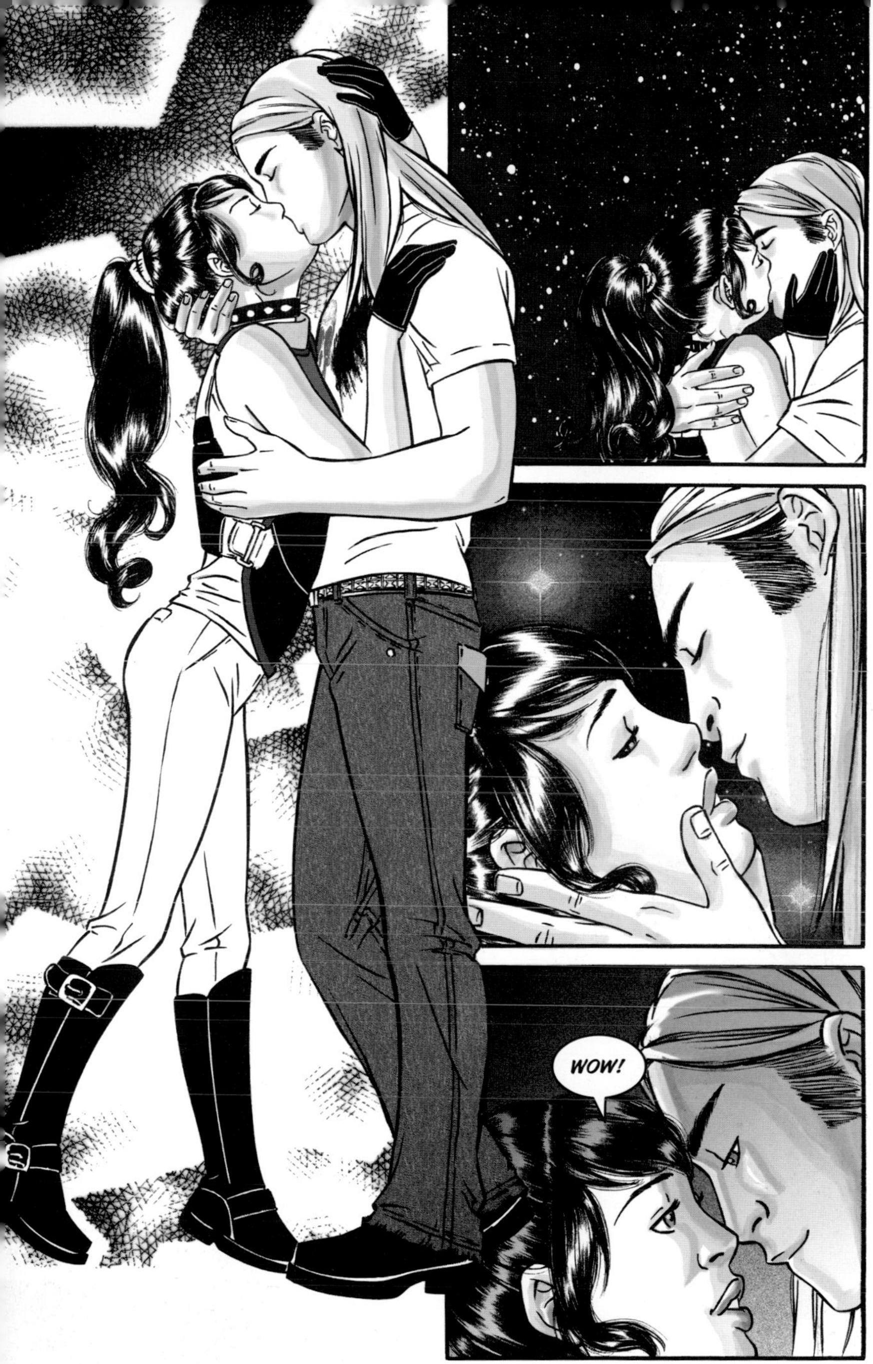
WOW!

102

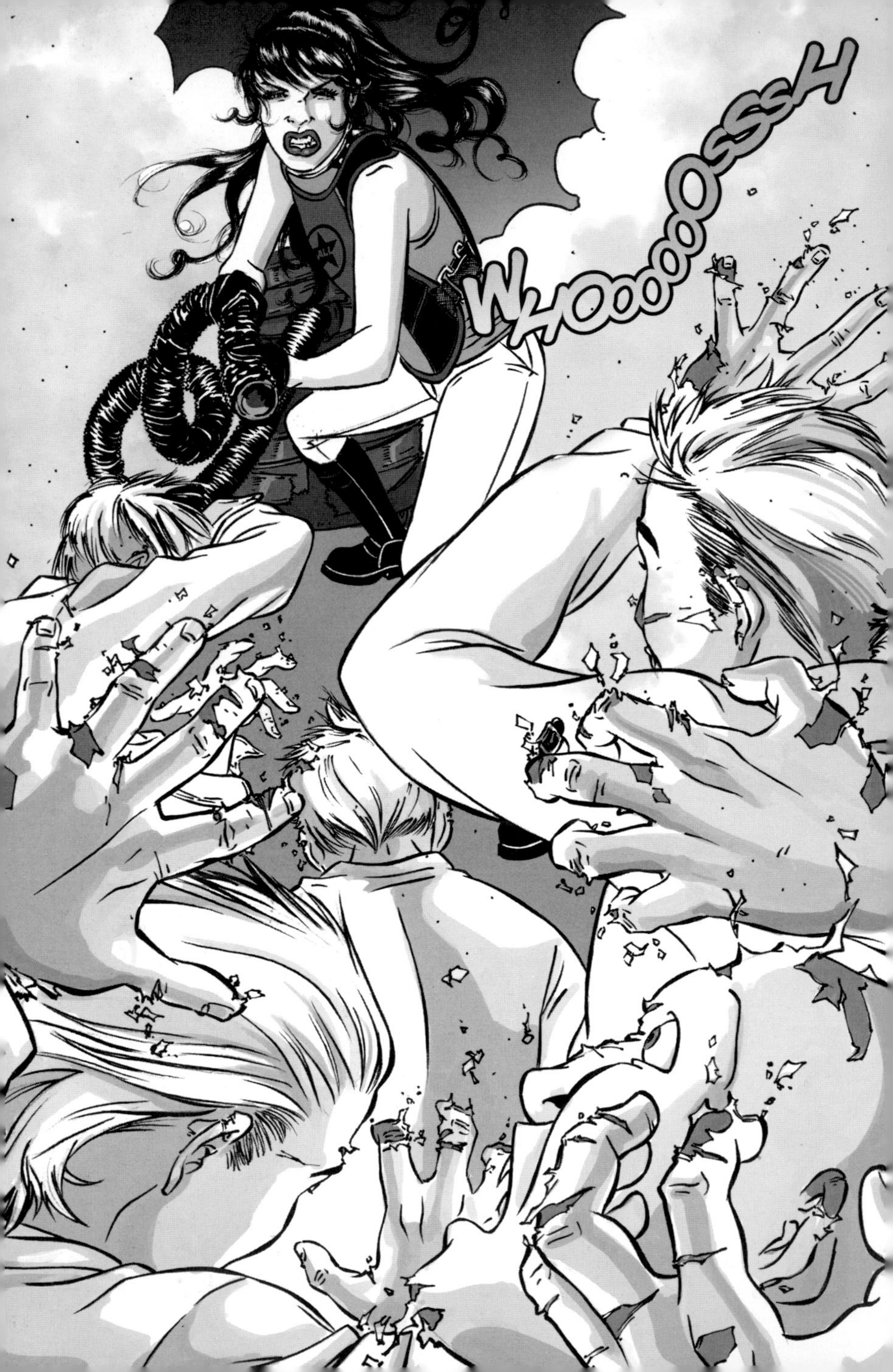
WHOOOOOOSSSH

114

115

117

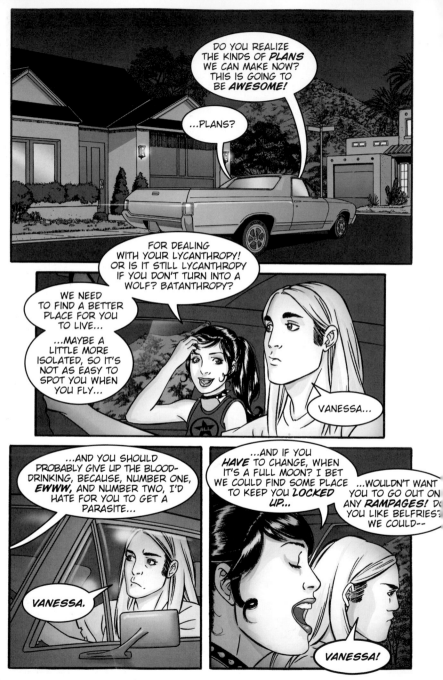

THAT SMARTS.

BUT MAYBE...

...THAT'S **SMART**?

YOU'RE, UH...YOU'RE *LEAVING*, AREN'T YOU?

MY COVER'S BLOWN. I KIND OF HAVE TO.

YOU'LL BE EIGHTEEN SOON ENOUGH.

YOUR PARENTS WILL COME CLEAN...AND SOMEONE WILL BE IN TOUCH.

SO...WILL I EVER SEE YOU AGAIN?

DEPENDS ON HOW MUCH TROUBLE YOU GET INTO.

HE DOESN'T SAY *GOOD-BYE*.

SOMEHOW THAT MAKES ME FEEL A LITTLE BETTER.

VANESSA SHINGLE, MONSTER HUNTER

MONSTERS EXPUNGED
ALL QUERIES WELCOME

Q. I heard you fought a vampire dressed as a clown! Clowns are terrifying.

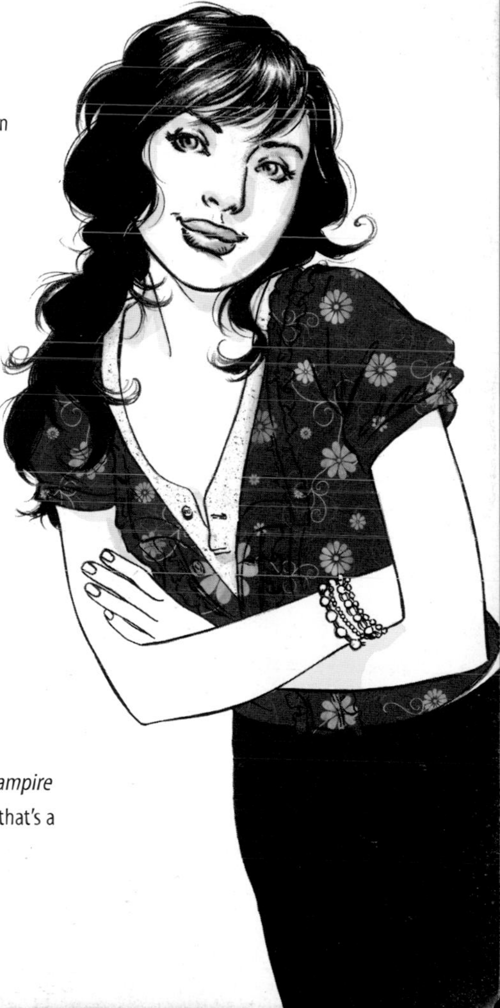

A. Well, there was a clown convention in Hackensack, and some of the attendees started disappearing, and then some bodies started turning up, and let me tell you, it's not easy dealing with a dead guy who's wearing a rainbow wig and a big red nose. I tried to feel for a pulse, and his big plastic lapel flower squirted me in the face. So I'm thinking, "Okay, what's the best way to figure out who the clown-killer vamp is?" and Stork was like, "You could go undercover," which was a pretty good idea—being a clown decoy, vamp bait to draw out the killer. So I did the whole thing with all the makeup and these enormous shoes, and it took a whole night of waiting around, but then—

—wait, are you talking about the *vampire* who was dressed like a clown? Because that's a whole other thing. Terrifying.

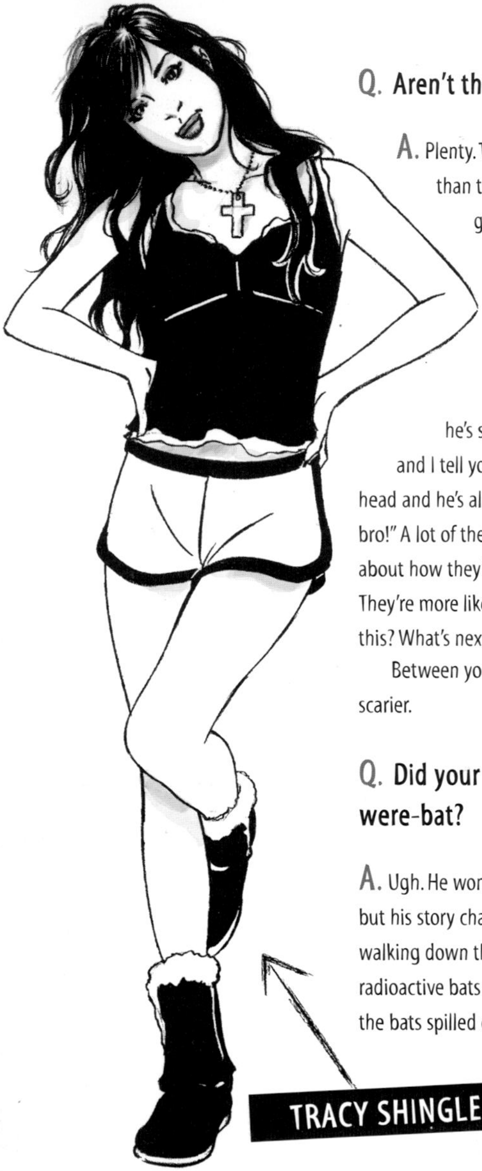
TRACY SHINGLE, VANESSA'S SISTER

Q. Aren't there any girl vampires?

A. Plenty. They're generally more subtle about it than the guys are, because, y'know, guys can get dumb sometimes. Okay, okay, not all guys. But a lot of guys don't think clearly once something like *I'm a vampire now!* happens to them. A guy gets turned into a vampire, and suddenly his skin clears up and he's standing taller and his muscles get big, and I tell you, it's like a switch gets flipped in his head and he's all, "Whooo! Look what I can do! High five, bro!" A lot of the girl vamps take more time to think about how they've changed, you know? What it means? They're more like, "Now what can I accomplish with all this? What's next?"

Between you and me, those girl vamps are a lot scarier.

Q. Did your boyfriend get bitten by a were-bat?

A. Ugh. He won't tell me. Or, I mean, he did tell me, but his story changes every time! One day it's, "I was walking down the street one night, and a truck full of radioactive bats was driving by and hit a pothole, and the bats spilled out and chewed all over me." But then

the next day it's, "The McClellan clan have been were-bats as far back as anybody can remember," like it's a hereditary thing or a family curse. Then I overheard him talking to what I'm pretty sure was his mom on the phone one day, and he said something like, "Ha ha, yeah, that was a really funny practical joke, you got me good with the whole bat thing." But maybe I misheard him.

Q. What happened to Mr. James?!! Is he all right? He didn't come back to school and he was the most decent teacher we had.

A. I was worried about him to begin with. I thought he should talk to a therapist or something, and I think he did have a talk with Mr. Barry, the school counselor. But it turns out he's pretty resilient. He just wanted to get away from town for a while. He sent me a couple of postcards, and I love his sense of humor, like, "Fresno is beautiful, despite the recently unearthed nest of ancient chthonic monsters. Wish you were here."

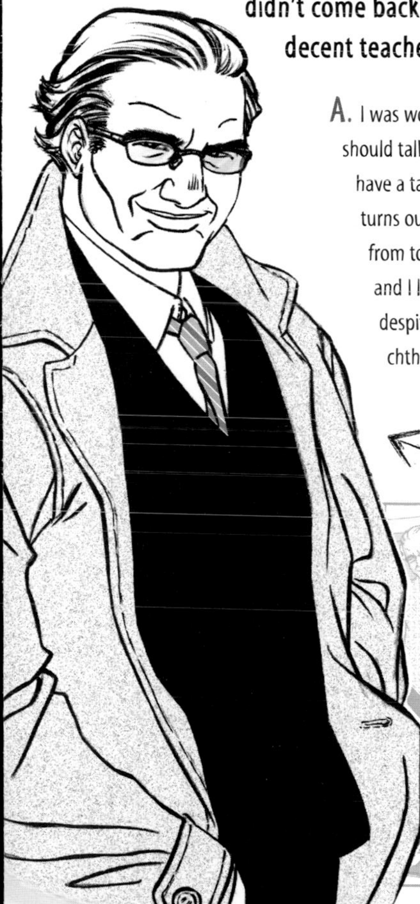

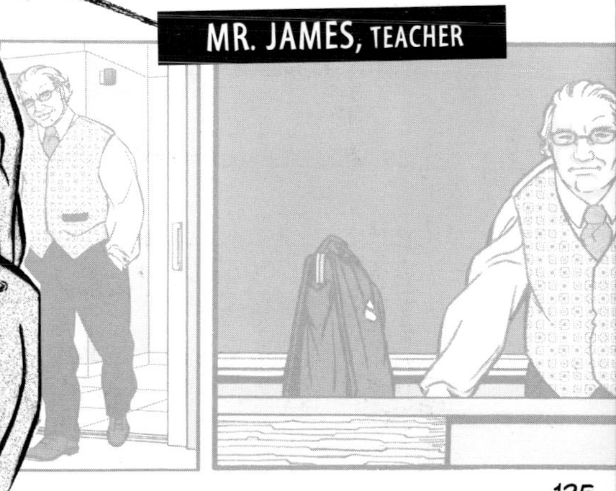

MR. JAMES, TEACHER

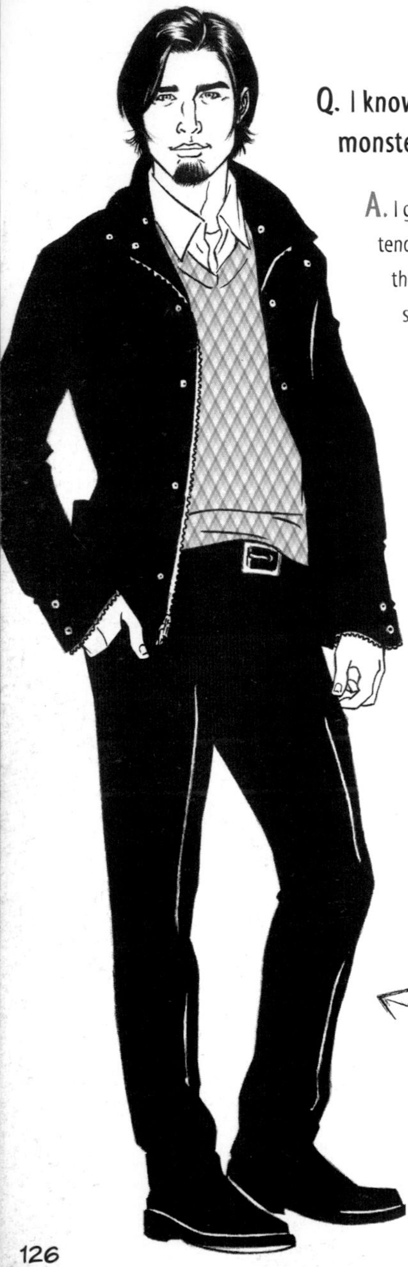

Q. I know vampires are bloodsucking monsters, but are they super hot?

A. I guess it depends on your point of view. They do tend to have really great hair and super-fit bodies, and they usually drive nice cars. And if you've got six or seven hundred years to work on it, you can really figure out what makes your date tick. But this is something that Stork and I talk about sometimes: how important it is not to ignore *red flags*. A red flag is something that you know is going to stop a relationship from moving forward, no matter how great everything else about it is. Say you meet a guy, and he's terrific, but then you find out he steals cars on the weekends. Red flag! Maybe you want to tell yourself, "Everything else about him is so great, I can overlook a little grand larceny." Take it from me, no, you can't. A red flag will ruin the relationship sooner or later. It can be exciting and all, but it's best not even to get involved in the first place. So you meet this tall, dark, handsome, rich, suave guy, and you tell yourself, "Maybe it's not such a big deal that he kills people and drinks their blood." RED FLAG! RED FLAG!

GARY BARRY, GUIDANCE COUNSELOR

Q. Is Jean-Paul your boyfriend? Isn't being a were-bat a red flag?

A. Maybe. Wait—I mean "maybe" about "is he my boyfriend," not the red flag. His *job* is to help people, he never hurts anybody but bad guys . . . so, no, being a were-bat is not a red flag. It's even like dating a cop. Um . . . *if* we were dating. I'm traveling all over the place, and he's all over the place too . . . but I guess we *are* dating, because whenever we wind up in the same city at the same time, we do hang out. Is he my boyfriend? Is my boyfriend a monster? I don't know! Next question!

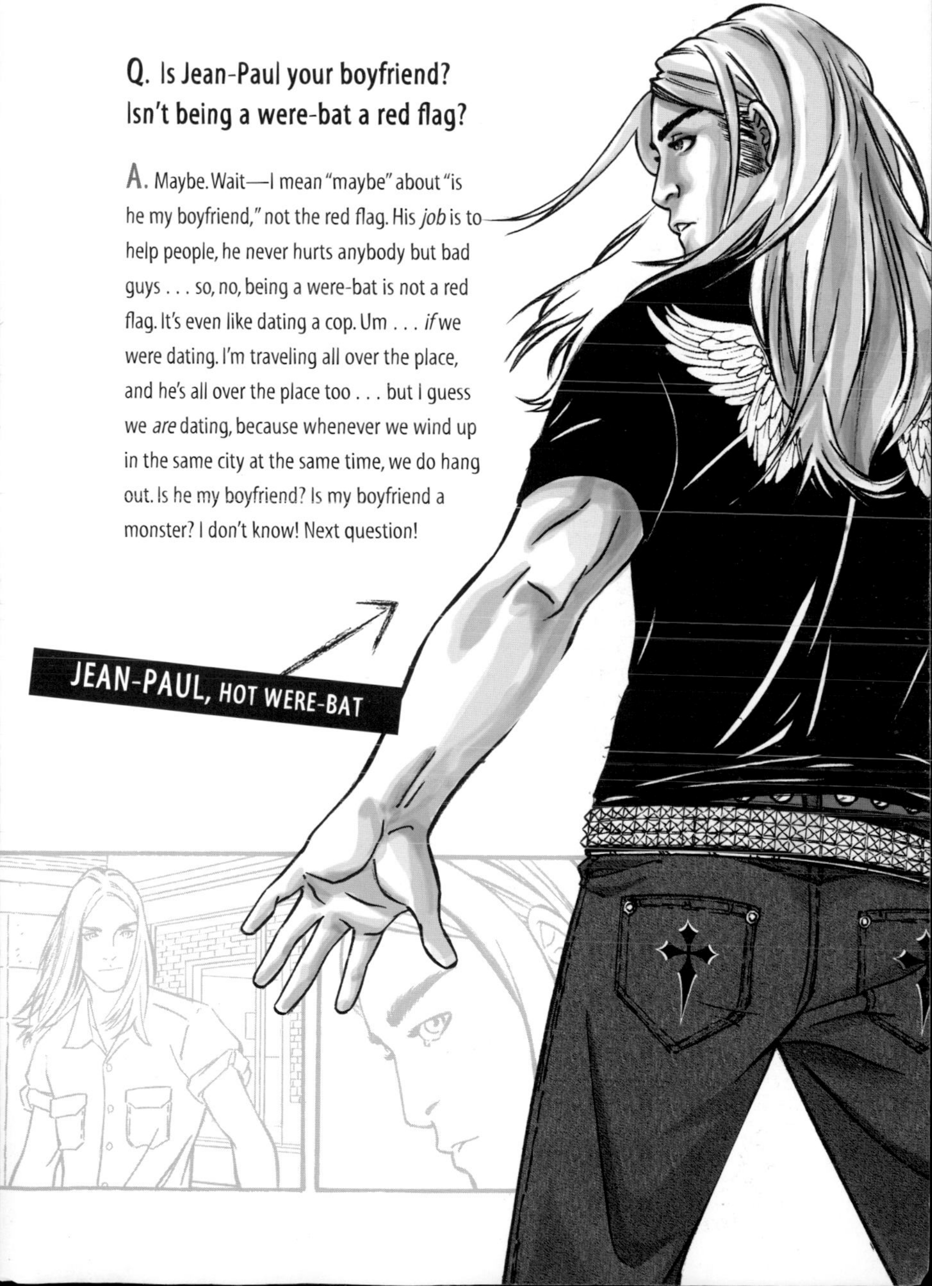

JEAN-PAUL, HOT WERE-BAT

ABOUT THE AUTHOR
AND THE ARTIST

Comic book author and video game writer DAN JOLLEY has created work for Marvel, DC, Dark Horse, and TokyoPop and for game developers including Activision and Ubisoft. He is also the author of several Graphic Myths and Legends titles including *Odysseus*, *Pigling* (a Korean Cinderella story), and *The Hero Twins: Against the Lords of Death* (a Mayan myth). Among his Twisted Journeys® titles are *Vampire Hunt*, *Escape from Pyramid X*, and *Agent Mongoose and the Hypno-Beam Scheme*. He lives in Georgia with his wife Tracy and three cats.

ALITHA MARTINEZ is a veteran in the world of mainstream American superhero comics who has ventured into manga as well. Her work can be found in issues of *Black Panther, Iron Man, Spider-Girl Battlebook: Streets of Fire, Shi, X-Men: Black Sun, Marvel Age: Fantastic Four, Voltron: Defender of the Universe*, and NBC's *Heroes*, as well as in her self-published series *Yume and Ever*. She is also the illustrator of Twisted Journeys® *Kung Fu Masters* and *The Quest for Dragon Mountain*. She lives in New York City.